JACK LONDON'S STORIES OF THE NORTH

Selected by Betty M. Owen
Introduction by Charles Rathbone

SCHOLASTIC INC.
New York Toronto London Auckland Sydney

No part of this publication may be reproduced in whole or in part, or stored in a retrieval system, or transmitted in any form or by any means, electronic, mechanical, photocopying, recording, or otherwise, without written permission of the publisher. For information regarding permission, write to Scholastic Inc., 730 Broadway, New York, NY 10003.

ISBN 0-590-42272-3

Copyright © 1965 by Scholastic Books, Inc. All rights reserved. Published by Scholastic Inc., 730 Broadway, New York, NY 10003, by arrangement with Irving Shepard.

12 11 10 9 8 7 6 5 4 3 2 1   10   8 9/8 0 1 2 3/9

Printed in the U.S.A.   01

CONTENTS

A WORD TO THE READER

IN A SENSE, there were three Jack Londons — London the man, London the philosopher, and London the story-teller. These tales of the frozen North certainly reveal the master storyteller, that deliberate craftsman whose unerring sense of the appropriate enabled him to perfect his special artistry of adventure. Adventure demands action, and action requires some adventurous agent to live aggressively and decisively, one who possesses both the spirit to dare and the courage to persevere. Just as his will to do what he chooses and his bold determination to be top dog literally force him into hard, competitive conflict with others of his kind, the violence he encounters there hardens his character, molding a lone, desperate being, generally cunning enough to trick his opponent, yet always strong enough to defeat him in direct combat when called upon to match blow for blow.

In all, he is a tough, egocentric individualist, a gambler who pushes himself beyond normal limits to attempt the impossible, who wagers his own life against an opportunity to achieve spectacular success. He hearkens to the call of the wild, and accepts the challenge of the unknown. For him no middle course is acceptable, no safe way attractive: his is the way of the unusual, the way of the heroic. And for this way, for this extreme gamble, he is willing to risk everything, even his life.

To this man, then, action is not only a natural part of life; it is a vitally necessary part. For it is only in moments of decisive activity that he can truly fulfill his role as agent of action, only during those periods of fevered agitation that he can become his true self. Similarly, he belongs in a special setting, in an environment which encourages violence and exploits fierce, competitive instincts. For this reason London often chose the exotic for a backdrop to his stories — either the wild savagery of the South Pacific or the bleak wasteland of the Yukon. But it takes more than mere ingredients to make a story work successfully: a writer must also have an extraordinary sense of pacing. Like a well-told detective story, a good tale of adventure must have a built-in narrative thrust, a deep-down movement that propels the characters, the plot, and the reader all toward one predetermined destination. When this drive is temporarily and skillfully blocked, the reader's curiosity is aroused, and suspense builds; when the block is finally removed, the reader feels answered, satisfied, relieved. Jack London the storyteller knew about suspense, just as he knew about action, for in his own personal life he had experienced plenty of both.

Jack London the man was born in 1876, the son of an unsuccessful California truck farmer. His early life was hard, and he grew up fast, soon becoming a wild, tough, restless young man, driven by an uneasy dissatisfaction with the present that characterized his entire life. By the age of twenty he had dropped out of high school, worked in a cannery, shipped out on a seal-hunting expedition, become a San Francisco Bay pirate, worked for the shore patrol that was busy chasing such pirates, sailed his own ship the sloop *Razzle Dazzle*, started working his way through college, and seen one of his own stories in print! The remainder of his life was to follow a similar pattern — always traveling, always changing, never satisfied with the *status quo*, never totally at rest.

He wrote as he lived — with a restless vigor. His talent was recognized remarkably early: at the age of seventeen a story took first prize in a contest sponsored by the San Francisco *Morning Call*; and at the height of his literary career, when he was selling every story he wrote and earning nearly $75,000 a year, he enjoyed a popularity that was truly international. Remembered especially for *The Call of the Wild* and *White Fang*, London wrote novels that were characterized by crisp description and by directness of narration. He always let his story tell itself, and carefully avoided artificial manipulation of his characters. Besides his short stories of life in the Northern wilds, he wrote of cannibals in the South Pacific, of misfortunate factory workers laboring in the dirty industrial cities at the turn of the century, of swashbuckling sailors and deep-sea fishermen, and — above all — of animals. He wrote plays and novels, murder mysteries and sermons, class-conscious socialistic essays and even an occasional venture into science fiction. He wrote steadily and voluminously until his death in 1916.

In both his life and in his writing, Jack London was a man of ideas as well as a man of action. Certainly he was a historian, a chronicler of that period in our history when the cry of "Gold!" still echoed on the Alaskan frontier, when the American "rags to riches" dream was still a reality. But more than mere reporter, he was also a serious thinker, a prober, a questioner. Though largely selfeducated, he became personally acquainted with the new psychological theories of Freud, who was attempting to describe and even explain what goes on within men's minds; and he dabbled in the complex "superman" philosophy of Friedrich Neitzsche. He knew the writings of Karl Marx, and became for a while an active crusader of socialist doctrine, an angry critic of capitalism. Of all his formal inquiries, however, it was those into Darwin's theories of evolution which most obviously left their mark. For Darwinism explained the world in terms of competition and conflict: "Survival of the fittest" was its byword. It saw man as only one of a multitude of organisms, each fighting the other for space, food, and survival. Interpreted by Jack London, this meant that, though the ordinary man was in no way specially provided for, there was real hope for the heroic, and great opportunity for the willful, the determined, and the courageous.

Thus by deliberately placing his characters in the most challenging of situations and then by submitting them to the most rigorous tests of physical, moral, and psychological endurance, London was able to pose those questions which would enable him to define that solitary adventurer with whom he had grown up, about whom he was always writing. What is will, or courage? How does a good man act when under ultimate stress? What can a man do on his own, without help, without gimmicks? How much cold, pain, or hunger can a man stand? How much does raw determination count in man's struggle to survive? What factors determine a man's breaking point? The answers London found are contained in his stories, in the very lives of the men and women and animals about whom he wrote.

Answers to these questions are to be found in the lives of London's characters. For they inhabit a world where the line is thin between fact and fiction and between life and literature, a world where London the thinker was able to join London the storyteller to explain to London the man who he was, and why.

The stories in this book reflect all three sides of London — the storyteller, the man, and the questioner. "To Build a Fire," "Love of Life," and "The Unexpected" all deal with people facing the challenge of hardship: one deals with death, one with hunger, and the third with the threat of madness. "The Son of the Wolf" and "The Story of Keesh" concern strategy of survival — the techniques of cunning that can mean swift victory or sudden death for those who face either the jaws of ferocious polar bears or the sharpened knives of jealous rivals. "The Sundog Trail" is an ingeniously constructed story of revenge, suspensefully and dramatically told in the best London tradition. The other three stories in this collection are about what happens when two totally different cultures come into conflict: "Nam-Bok the Unveracious" and "The White Man's Way" both concern the reactions of Eskimos when confronted by the incredibly strange and downright frightening world of the white fur traders of the south; "The Wife of a King" is the tale of a Klondike Pygmalion, a sort of Yukon *My Fair Lady*. They are all carefully worked-out tales of action and adventure, stories well told to keep the reader in suspense. Still, they offer sufficient ideas about what man really is and what he is able to do under stress to merit a second or third reading. Whether read all together or one at a time, these stories will excite your imagination and hold it long after you have put the book down.

Charles Rathbone
North Haven High School
North Haven, Connecticut

THE WHITE
MAN'S WAY

1

"To cook by your fire and to sleep under your roof for the night," I had announced on entering old Ebbits's cabin; and he had looked at me blear-eyed and vacuous, while Zilla had favored me with a sour face and a contemptuous grunt. Zilla was his wife, and no more bitter-tongued, implacable old squaw dwelt on the Yukon. Nor would I have stopped there had my dogs been less tired or had the rest of the village been inhabited. But this cabin alone had I found occupied, so in this cabin, I took my shelter.

Old Ebbits now and again pulled his tangled wits together, and hints and sparkles of intelligence came and went in his eyes. Several times during the preparation of my supper he even essayed hospitable inquiries about my health, the condition and number of my dogs, and the distance I had traveled that day. And each time Zilla had looked sourer than ever and grunted more contemptuously.

Yet I confess that there was no particular call for cheerfulness on their part. There they crouched by the fire, the pair of them, at the end of their days, old and withered and helpless, racked by rheumatism, bitten by hunger, and tantalized by the frying odors of my abundance of meat. They rocked back and forth in a slow and hopeless way, and regularly, once every five minutes, Ebbits emitted a low groan. It was not so much a groan of pain, as of pain weariness. He was oppressed by the weight and the torment of this thing called life, and still more was he oppressed by the fear of death. His was that eternal tragedy of the aged, from whom the joy of life has departed and the instinct for death has not come.

When my moose meat spluttered rowdily in the frying pan, I noticed old Ebbits's nostrils twitch and distend as he caught the food scent. He ceased rocking for a space and forgot to groan, while a look of intelligence seemed to come into his face.

Zilla, on the other hand, rocked more rapidly, and for the first time, in sharp little yelps, voiced her pain. It came to me that their behavior was like that of hungry dogs, and in the fitness of things I should not have been astonished had Zilla suddenly developed a tail and thumped it on the floor in right doggish fashion. Ebbits drooled a little and stopped his rocking very frequently to lean forward and thrust his tremulous nose nearer to the source of gustatory excitement.

When I passed them each a plate of the fried meat, they ate greedily, making loud mouth noises — champings of worn teeth and sucking intakes of breath, accompanied by a continuous spluttering and mumbling. After that, when I gave them each a mug of scalding tea, the noises ceased. Easement and content came into their faces. Zilla relaxed her sour mouth long enough to sigh her satisfaction. Neither rocked any more, and they seemed to have fallen into placid meditation. Then a dampness came into Ebbits's eyes, and I knew that the sorrow of self-pity was his. The search required to find their pipes told plainly that they had been without tobacco a long time, and the old man's eagerness for it rendered him helpless, so that I was compelled to light his pipe for him.

"Why are you all alone in the village?" I asked. "Is everybody dead? Has there been a great sickness? Are you alone left of the living?"

Old Ebbits shook his head, saying: "Nay, there

3

has been no great sickness. The village has gone away to hunt meat. We be too old, our legs are not strong, nor can our backs carry the burdens of camp and trail. Wherefore we remain here and wonder when the young men will return with meat."

"What if the young men do return with meat?" Zilla demanded harshly.

"They may return with much meat," he quavered hopefully.

"Even so, with much meat," she continued, more harshly than before. "But of what worth to you and me? A few bones to gnaw in our toothless old age. But the back fat, the kidneys, and the tongues — these shall go into other mouths than thine and mine, old man."

Ebbits nodded his head and wept silently.

"There be no one to hunt meat for us," she cried, turning fiercely upon me.

There was accusation in her manner, and I shrugged my shoulders in token that I was not guilty of the unknown crime imputed to me.

"Know, O White Man, that it is because of thy kind, because of all white men, that my man and I have no meat in our old age and sit without tobacco in the cold."

"Nay," Ebbits said gravely, with a stricter sense

of justice. "Wrong has been done us, it be true; but the white men did not mean the wrong."

"Where be Moklan?" she demanded. "Where be thy strong son, Moklan, and the fish he was ever willing to bring that you might eat?"

The old man shook his head.

"And where be Bidarshik, thy strong son? Ever was he a mighty hunter, and ever did he bring thee the good back fat and the sweet dried tongues of the moose and the caribou. I see no back fat and no sweet dried tongues. Your stomach is full with emptiness through the days, and it is for a man of a very miserable and lying people to give you to eat."

"Nay," old Ebbits interposed in kindliness, "the white man's is not a lying people. The white man speaks true. Always does the white man speak true." He paused, casting about him for words wherewith to temper the severity of what he was about to say. "But the white man speaks true in different ways. Today he speaks true one way, tomorrow he speaks true another way, and there is no understanding him nor his way."

"Today speak true one way, tomorrow speak true another way, which is to lie," was Zilla's dictum.

"There is no understanding the white man," Ebbits went on doggedly.

5

The meat, and the tea, and the tobacco seemed to have brought him back to life, and he gripped tighter hold of the idea behind his age-bleared eyes. He straightened up somewhat. His voice lost its querulous and whimpering note and became strong and positive. He turned upon me with dignity, and addressed me as equal addresses equal.

"The white man's eyes are not shut," he began. "The white man sees all things, and thinks greatly, and is very wise. But the white man of one day is not the white man of next day, and there is no understanding him. He does not do things always in the same way. And what way his next way is to be, one cannot know. Always does the Indian do the one thing in the one way. Always does the moose come down from the high mountains when the winter is here. Always does the salmon come in the spring when the ice has gone out of the river. Always does everything do all things in the same way, and the Indian knows and understands. But the white man does not do all things in the same way, and the Indian does not know nor understand.

"Tobacco be very good. It be food to the hungry man. It makes the strong man stronger, and the angry man to forget that he is angry. Also is tobacco of value. It is of very great value. The Indian give one large salmon for one leaf of tobacco, and he chews the tobacco for a long time. It is the juice of the tobacco that is good. When it runs down his throat it makes him feel good inside. But the white man! When his mouth is full with the juice, what does he do? That juice, that juice of great value, he spits it out in the snow and it is lost. Does the white man like tobacco? I do not know. But if he likes tobacco, why does he spit out its value and lose it in the snow? It is a great foolishness and without understanding."

He ceased, puffed at the pipe, found that it was out, and passed it over to Zilla, who took the sneer at the white man off her lips in order to pucker them about the pipe stem. Ebbits seemed sinking back into his senility with the tale untold, and I demanded:

"What of thy sons, Moklan and Bidarshik? And why is it that you and your old woman are without meat at the end of your years?"

He roused himself as from sleep and straightened up with an effort.

"It is not good to steal," he said. "When the dog takes your meat you beat the dog with a club. Such is the law. It is the law the man gave to the dog, and the dog must live to the law, else will it suffer the pain of the club. When man takes your meat, or your canoe, or your wife, you kill that man. That is the law, and it is a good law. It is not good

7

to steal, wherefore it is the law that the man who steals must die. Whoso breaks the law must suffer hurt. It is a great hurt to die."

"But if you kill the man, why do you not kill the dog?" I asked.

Old Ebbits looked at me in childlike wonder, while Zilla sneered openly at the absurdity of my question.

"It is the way of the white man," Ebbits mumbled with an air of resignation.

"It is the foolishness of the white man," snapped Zilla.

"Then let old Ebbits teach the white man wisdom," I said softly.

"The dog is not killed, because it must pull the sled of the man. No man pulls another man's sled, wherefore the man is killed."

"Oh," I murmured.

"That is the law," old Ebbits went on. "Now listen, O White Man, and I will tell you of a great foolishness. There is an Indian. His name is Mobits. From white man he steals two pounds of flour. What does the white man do? Does he beat Mobits? No. Does he kill Mobits? No. What does he do to Mobits? I will tell you, O White Man. He has a house. He puts Mobits in that house. The roof is good. The walls are thick. He makes a fire that Mobits may be warm. He gives Mobits plenty grub to eat. It is good grub. Never in all his days does Mobits eat so good grub. There is bacon, and bread, and beans without end. Mobits have very good time.

"There is a big lock on door so that Mobits does not run away. This also is a great foolishness. Mobits will not run away. All the time is there plenty grub in that place, and warm blankets, and a big fire. Very foolish to run away. Mobits is not foolish. Three months Mobits stop in that place. He steal two pounds of flour. For that, white man take plenty good care of him. Mobits eat many pounds of flour, many pounds of sugar, of bacon, of beans without end. Also, Mobits drink much tea. After three months white man open door and tell Mobits he must go. Mobits does not want to go. He is like dog that is fed long time in one place. He want to stay in that place, and the white man must drive Mobits away. So Mobits come back to this village, and he is very fat. That is the white man's way, and there is no understanding it. It is a foolishness, a great foolishness."

"But thy sons?" I insisted. "Thy very strong sons and thine old-age hunger?"

"There was Moklan," Ebbits began.

"A strong man," interrupted the mother. "He could dip paddle all of a day and night and never stop for the need of rest. He was wise in the way

9

of the salmon and in the way of the water. He was very wise."

"There was Moklan," Ebbits repeated, ignoring the interruption. "In the spring, he went down the Yukon with the young men to trade at Cambell Fort. There is a post there, filled with the goods of the white man, and a trader whose name is Jones. Likewise is there a white man's medicine man, what you call missionary. Also is there bad water at Cambell Fort, where the Yukon goes slim like a maiden, and the water is fast, and the currents rush this way and that and come together, and there are whirls and sucks, and always are the currents changing and the face of the water changing, so at any two times it is never the same. Moklan is my son, wherefore he is brave man —"

"Was not my father brave man?" Zilla demanded.

"Thy father was brave man," Ebbits acknowledged, with the air of one who will keep peace in the house at any cost. "Moklan is thy son and mine, wherefore he is brave. Mayhap, because of thy very brave father, Moklan is too brave. It is like when too much water is put in the pot it spills over. So too much bravery is put into Moklan, and the bravery spills over.

"The young men are much afraid of the bad water at Cambell Fort. But Moklan is not afraid.

He laughs strong, Ho! ho! and he goes forth into the bad water. But where the currents come together the canoe is turned over. A whirl takes Moklan by the legs, and he goes around and around, and down and down, and is seen no more."

"Ai! ai!" wailed Zilla. "Crafty and wise was he, and my first-born!"

"I am the father of Moklan," Ebbits said, having patiently given the woman space for her noise. "I get into canoe and journey down to Cambell Fort to collect the debt!"

"Debt!" I interrupted. "What debt?"

"The debt of Jones, who is chief trader," came the answer. "Such is the law of travel in a strange country."

I shook my head in token of my ignorance, and Ebbits looked compassion at me, while Zilla snorted her customary contempt.

"Look you, O White Man," he said. "In thy camp is a dog that bites. When the dog bites a man, you give that man a present because you are sorry and because it is thy dog. You make payment. Is it not so? Also, if you have in thy country bad hunting, or bad water, you must make payment. It is just. It is the law. Did not my father's brother go over into the Tanana Country and get killed by a bear? And did not the Tanana tribe pay my father many blankets and fine furs? It

11

was just. It was bad hunting, and the Tanana people made payment for the bad hunting.

"So I, Ebbits, journeyed down to Cambell Fort to collect the debt. Jones, who is chief trader, looked at me, and he laughed. He made great laughter, and would not give payment. I went to the medicine man, what you call missionary, and had large talk about the bad water and the payment that should be mine. And the missionary made talk about other things. He talk about where Moklan has gone, now he is dead. There be large fires in that place, and if missionary make true talk, I know that Moklan will be cold no more. Also the missionary talk about where I shall go when I am dead. And he say bad things. He say that I am blind. Which is a lie. He say that I am in great darkness. Which is a lie. And I say that the day come and the night come for everybody just the same, and that in my village it is no more dark than at Cambell Fort. Also, I say that darkness and light and where we go when we die be different things from the matter of payment of just debt for bad water. Then the missionary make large anger, and call me bad names of darkness, and tell me to go away. And so I come back from Cambell Fort, and no payment has been made, and Moklan is dead, and in my old age I am without fish and meat."

"Because of the white man," said Zilla.

"Because of the white man," Ebbits concurred. "And other things because of the white man. There was Bidarshik. One way did the white man deal with him; and yet another way for the same thing did the white man deal with Yamikan. And first must I tell you of Yamikan, who was a young man of this village and who chanced to kill a white man. It is not good to kill a man of another people. Always is there great trouble. It was not the fault of Yamikan that he killed the white man. Yamikan spoke always soft words and ran away from wrath as a dog from a stick. But this white man drank much whiskey, and in the nighttime came to Yamikan's house and made much fight. Yamikan cannot run away, and the white man tries to kill him. Yamikan does not like to die, so he kills the white man.

"Then is all the village in great trouble. We are much afraid that we must make large payment to the white man's people, and we hide our blankets, and our furs, and all our wealth, so that it will seem that we are poor people and can make only small payment. After long time white men come. They are soldier white men, and they take Yamikan away with them. His mother make great noise and throw ashes in her hair, for she knows Yamikan is dead.

13

And all the village knows that Yamikan is dead, and is glad that no payment is asked.

"That is in the spring when the ice has gone out of the river. One year go by, two years go by. It is springtime again, and the ice has gone out of the river. And then Yamikan, who is dead, comes back to us, and he is not dead, but very fat, and we know that he has slept warm and had plenty grub to eat. He has much fine clothes and is all the same white man, and he has gathered large wisdom so that he is very quick head man in the village.

"And he has strange things to tell of the way of the white man, for he has seen much of the white man and done a great travel into the white man's country. First place, soldier white men take him down the river long way. All the way do they take him down the river to the end, where it runs into a lake which is larger than all the land and large as the sky. I do not know the Yukon is so big river, but Yamikan has seen with his own eyes. I do not think there is a lake larger than all the land and large as the sky, but Yamikan has seen. Also, he has told me that the waters of this lake be salt, which is a strange thing and beyond understanding.

"But the White Man knows all these marvels for himself, so I shall not weary him with the telling of them. Only will I tell him what happened to

14

Yamikan. The white man give Yamikan much fine grub. All the time does Yamikan eat, and all the time is there plenty more grub. The white man lives under the sun, so said Yamikan, where there be much warmth, and animals have only hair and no fur, and the green things grow large and strong and become flour, and beans, and potatoes. And under the sun there is never famine. Always is there plenty grub. I do not know. Yamikan has said.

"And here is a strange thing that befell Yamikan. Never did the white man hurt him. Only did they give him warm bed at night and plenty fine grub. They take him across the salt lake which is big as the sky. He is on white man's fireboat, what you call steamboat, only he is on boat maybe twenty times bigger than steamboat on Yukon. Also, it is made of iron, this boat, and yet does it not sink. This I do not understand, but Yamikan has said, 'I have journeyed far on the iron boat; behold! I am still alive.' It is a white man's soldier-boat with many soldier men upon it.

"After many sleeps of travel, a long, long time, Yamikan comes to a land where there is no snow. I cannot believe this. It is not in the nature of things that when winter comes there shall be no snow. But Yamikan has seen. Also have I asked the white men, and they have said yes, there is no snow in that country. But I cannot believe, and now I ask you if snow never come in that country. Also, I would hear the name of that country. I have heard the name before, but I would hear it again, if it be the same — thus will I know if I have heard lies or true talk."

Old Ebbits regarded me with a wistful face. He would have the truth at any cost, though it was his desire to retain his faith in the marvel he had never seen.

"Yes," I answered, "it is true talk that you have heard. There is no snow in that country, and its name is California."

"Cal-ee-forn-ee-yeh," he mumbled twice and thrice, listening intently to the sound of the syllables as they fell from his lips. He nodded his head in confirmation. "Yes, it is the same country of which Yamikan made talk."

I recognized the adventure of Yamikan as one likely to occur in the early days when Alaska first passed into the possession of the United States. Such a murder case, occurring before the instalment of territorial law and officials, might well have been taken down to the United States for trial before a federal court.

"When Yamikan is in this country where there is no snow," old Ebbits continued, "he is taken to large house where many men make much talk.

16

Long time men talk. Also many questions do they ask Yamikan. By and by they tell Yamikan he have no more trouble. Yamikan does not understand, for never has he had any trouble. All the time have they given him warm place to sleep and plenty grub.

"But after that they give him much better grub, and they give him money, and they take him many places in white man's country, and he sees many strange things which are beyond the understanding of Ebbits, who is an old man and has not journeyed far. After two years, Yamikan comes back to this village, and he is head man, and very wise until he dies.

"But before he dies, many times does he sit by my fire and make talk of the strange things he has seen. And Bidarshik, who is my son, sits by the fire and listens; and his eyes are very wide and large because of the things he hears. One night, after Yamikan has gone home, Bidarshik stands up, so, very tall, and he strikes his chest with his fist, and says, 'When I am a man, I shall journey in far places, even to the land where there is no snow, and see things for myself.'"

"Always did Bidarshik journey in far places," Zilla interrupted proudly.

"It be true," Ebbits assented gravely. "And always did he return to sit by the fire and hunger for yet other and unknown far places."

"And always did he remember the salt lake as big as the sky and the country under the sun where there is no snow," quoth Zilla.

"And always did he say, 'When I have the full strength of a man, I will go and see for myself if the talk of Yamikan be true talk,'" said Ebbits.

"But there was no way to go to the white man's country," said Zilla.

"Did he not go down to the salt lake that is big as the sky?" Ebbits demanded.

"And there was no way for him across the salt lake," said Zilla.

"Save in the white man's fireboat which is of iron and is bigger than twenty steamboats on the Yukon," said Ebbits. He scowled at Zilla, whose withered lips were again writhing into speech, and compelled her to silence. "But the white man would not let him cross the salt lake in the fireboat, and he returned to sit by the fire and hunger for the country under the sun where there is no snow."

"Yet on the salt lake had he seen the fireboat of iron that did not sink," cried out Zilla the irrepressible.

"Ay," said Ebbits, "and he saw that Yamikan had made true talk of the things he had seen. But there was no way for Bidarshik to journey to the white man's land under the sun, and he grew sick and weary like an old man and moved not away from the fire. No longer did he go forth to kill meat —"

"And no longer did he eat the meat placed before him," Zilla broke in. "He would shake his head and say, 'Only do I care to eat the grub of the white man and grow fat after the manner of Yamikan.'"

"And he did not eat the meat," Ebbits went on. "And the sickness of Bidarshik grew into a great sickness until I thought he would die. It was not a sickness of the body, but of the head. It was a sickness of desire. I, Ebbits, who am his father, make a great think. I have no more sons and I do not want Bidarshik to die. It is a head sickness, and there is but one way to make it well. Bidarshik must journey across the lake as large as the sky to the land where there is no snow, else will he die. I make a very great think, and then I see the way for Bidarshik to go.

"So, one night when he sits by the fire, very sick, his head hanging down, I say, 'My son, I have learned the way for you to go to the white man's land.' He looks at me, and his face is glad. 'Go,' I say, 'even as Yamikan went.' But Bidarshik is sick and does not understand. 'Go forth,' I say, 'and find a white man, and, even as Yamikan, do

19

you kill that white man. Then will the soldier white men come and get you, and even as they took Yamikan will they take you across the salt lake to the white man's land. And then, even as Yamikan, will you return very fat, your eyes full of the things you have seen, your head filled with wisdom.'

"And Bidarshik stands up very quick, and his hand is reaching out for his gun. 'Where do you go?' I ask. 'To kill the white man,' he says. And I see that my words have been good in the ears of Bidarshik and that he will grow well again. Also do I know that my words have been wise.

"There is a white man come to this village. He does not seek after gold in the ground, nor after furs in the forest. All the time does he seek after bugs and flies. He does not eat the bugs and flies, then why does he seek after them? I do not know. Only do I know that he is a funny white man. Also does he seek after the eggs of birds. He does not eat the eggs. All that is inside he takes out, and only does he keep the shell. Eggshell is not good to eat. Nor does he eat the eggshell, but puts them away in soft boxes where they will not break. He catch many small birds. But he does not eat the birds. He takes only the skins and puts them away in boxes. Also does he like bones. Bones are not good to eat. And this strange white man likes

best the bones of long time ago which he digs out
of the ground.

"But he is not a fierce white man, and I know
he will die very easy; so I say to Bidarshik, 'My son,
there is the white man for you to kill.' And Bidarshik says that my words be wise. So he goes to a
place he knows where are many bones in the
ground. He digs up very many of these bones and
brings them to the strange white man's camp. The
white man is made very glad. His face shines like
the sun, and he smiles with much gladness as he
looks at the bones. He bends his head over, so, to
look well at the bones, and then Bidarshik strikes
him hard on the head, with axe, once, so, and the
strange white man kicks and is dead.

"'Now,' I say to Bidarshik, 'will the white soldier
men come and take you away to the land under the
sun, where you will eat much and grow fat.' Bidarshik is happy. Already has his sickness gone from
him, and he sits by the fire and waits for the coming
of the white soldier men.

"How was I to know the way of the white
man is never twice the same?" the old man demanded, whirling upon me fiercely. "How was I
to know that what the white man does yesterday
he will not do today, and that what he does today
he will not do tomorrow?" Ebbits shook his head
sadly. "There is no understanding the white man.

21

Yesterday he takes Yamikan to the land under the sun and makes him fat with much grub. Today he takes Bidarshik and — what does he do with Bidarshik? Let me tell you what he does with Bidarshik.

"I, Ebbits, his father, will tell you. He takes Bidarshik to Cambell Fort, and he ties a rope around his neck, so, and, when his feet are no more on the ground, he dies."

"Ail ail" wailed Zilla. "And never does he cross the lake large as the sky, nor see the land under the sun where there is no snow."

"Wherefore," old Ebbits said with grave dignity, "there be no one to hunt meat for me in my old age, and I sit hungry by my fire and tell my story to the White Man who has given me grub, and strong tea, and tobacco for my pipe."

"Because of the lying and very miserable white people," Zilla proclaimed shrilly.

"Nay," answered the old man with gentle positiveness. "Because of the way of the white man, which is without understanding and never twice the same."

THE STORY
OF KEESH

2

KEESH lived long ago on the rim of the polar
sea, was head man of his village through
many and prosperous years, and died full of honors
with his name on the lips of men. So long ago
did he live that only the old men remember his
name, his name and the tale, which they got
from the old men before them, and which the
old men to come will tell to their children and
their children's children down to the end of
time. And the winter darkness, when the north
gales make their long sweep across the ice pack,
and the air is filled with flying white, and no
man may venture forth, is the chosen time for

the telling of how Keesh, from the poorest igloo in the village, rose to power and place over them all.

He was a bright boy, so the tale runs, healthy and strong, and he had seen thirteen suns, in their way of reckoning time. For each winter the sun leaves the land in darkness, and the next year a new sun returns so that they may be warm again and look upon one another's faces. The father of Keesh had been a very brave man, but he had met his death in a time of famine, when he sought to save the lives of his people by taking the life of a great polar bear. In his eagerness he came to close grapples with the bear, and his bones were crushed; but the bear had much meat on him and the people were saved. Keesh was his only son, and after that Keesh lived alone with his mother. But the people are prone to forget, and they forgot the deed of his father; and he being but a boy, and his mother only a woman, they, too, were swiftly forgotten, and ere long came to live in the meanest of all the igloos.

It was at a council one night in the big igloo of Klosh-Kwan, the chief, that Keesh showed the blood that ran in his veins and the manhood that stiffened his back. With the dignity of an elder he rose to his feet and waited for silence amid the babble of voices.

"It is true that meat be apportioned me and mine," he said. "But it is ofttimes old and tough, this meat, and, moreover, it has an unusual quantity of bones."

The hunters, grizzled and gray, and lusty and young, were aghast. The like had never been known before. A child that talked like a grown man, and said harsh things to their very faces!

But steadily and with seriousness Keesh went on. "For that I know my father, Bok, was a great hunter, I speak these words. It is said that Bok brought home more meat than any of the two best hunters, that with his own hands he attended to the division of it, that with his own eyes he saw to it that the least old woman and the least old man received fair share."

"Na! Na!" the men cried. "Put the child out!" "Send him off to bed!" "He is no man that he should talk to men and graybeards!"

He waited calmly till the uproar died down.

"Thou hast a wife, Ugh-Gluk," he said, "and for her dost thou speak. And thou, too, Massuk, a mother also; and for them dost thou speak. My mother has no one, save me; wherefore I speak. As I say, though Bok be dead because he hunted over-keenly, it is just that I, who am his son, and that Ikeega, who is my mother and was his wife, should have meat in plenty so long as there be

25

meat in plenty in the tribe. I, Keesh, the son of Bok, have spoken."

He sat down, his ears keenly alert to the flood of protest and indignation his words had created.

"That a boy should speak in council!" old Ugh-Gluk was mumbling.

"Shall the babes in arms tell us men the things we shall do?" Massuk demanded in a loud voice. "Am I a man that I should be made a mock by every child that cries for meat?"

The anger boiled to a white heat. They ordered him to bed, threatened that he should have no meat at all, and promised him sore beatings for his presumption. Keesh's eyes began to flash, and the blood to pound darkly under his skin. In the midst of the abuse he sprang to his feet.

"Hear me, ye men!" he cried. "Never shall I speak in the council again, never again till the men come to me and say, 'It is well, Keesh, that thou shouldst speak; it is well and it is our wish.' Take this now, ye men, for my last word. Bok, my father, was a great hunter. I too, his son, shall go and hunt the meat that I eat. And be it known, now, that the division of that which I kill shall be fair. And no widow nor weak one shall cry in the night because there is no meat, when the strong men are groaning in great pain for that they have eaten overmuch. And in the days to come there shall be shame upon the strong men who have eaten overmuch. I, Keesh, have said it!"

Jeers and scornful laughter followed him out of the igloo, but his jaw was set and he went his way, looking neither to right nor left.

The next day he went forth along the shore line where the ice and the land met together. Those who saw him go noted that he carried his bow, with a goodly supply of bone-barbed arrows, and that across his shoulder was his father's big hunting spear. And there was laughter, and much talk, at the event. It was an unprecedented occurrence. Never did boys of his tender age go forth to hunt, much less to hunt alone. Also were there shaking of heads and prophetic mutterings, and the women looked pityingly at Ikeega, and her face was grave and sad.

"He will be back ere long," they said cheeringly.

"Let him go; it will teach him a lesson," the hunters said. "And he will come back shortly, and he will be meek and soft of speech in the days to follow."

But a day passed, and a second, and on the third a wild gale blew, and there was no Keesh. Ikeega tore her hair and put soot of the seal oil on her face in token of her grief; and the women assailed the men with bitter words in that they had mistreated the boy and sent him to his death; and the men made no answer, preparing to go in search of the body when the storm abated.

Early next morning, however, Keesh strode into the village. But he came not shamefacedly. Across his shoulders he bore a burden of fresh-killed meat. And there was importance in his step and arrogance in his speech.

"Go, ye men, with the dogs and sledges, and take my trail for the better part of a day's travel," he said. "There is much meat on the ice—a she-bear and two half-grown cubs."

Ikeega was overcome with joy, but he received her demonstrations in manlike fashion, saying: "Come, Ikeega, let us eat. And after that I shall sleep, for I am weary."

And he passed into their igloo and ate profoundly, and after that slept for twenty running hours.

There was much doubt at first, much doubt and discussion. The killing of a polar bear is very dangerous, but thrice dangerous is it, and three times thrice, to kill a mother bear with her cubs. The men could not bring themselves to believe that the boy Keesh, single-handed, had accomplished so great a marvel. But the women spoke of the fresh-killed meat he had brought on his back, and this was an overwhelming argument against their unbelief. So they finally departed, grumbling greatly that in all probability, if the thing were so, he had neglected to cut up the carcasses. Now in the north it is very necessary that this should be done as soon as a kill is made. If not, the meat freezes so solidly as to turn the edge of the sharpest knife, and a three-hundred-pound bear, frozen stiff, is no easy thing to put upon a sled and haul over the rough ice. But arrived at the spot, they found not only the kill which they had doubted, but that Keesh had quartered the beasts in true hunter fashion, and removed the entrails.

Thus began the mystery of Keesh, a mystery that deepened and deepened with the passing of the days. His very next trip he killed a young bear, nearly full-grown, and on the trip following, a large male bear and his mate. He was ordinarily gone from three to four days, though it was nothing unusual for him to stay away a week at a time on the ice field. Always he declined company on these expeditions, and the people marveled. "How does he do it?" they demanded of one another. "Never does he take a dog with him, and dogs are of such great help, too."

"Why dost thou hunt only bear?" Klosh-Kwan once ventured to ask.

And Keesh made fitting answer. "It is well known that there is more meat on the bear," he said.

But there was also talk of witchcraft in the

village. "He hunts with evil spirits," some of the people contended, "wherefore his hunting is rewarded. How else can it be, save that he hunts with evil spirits?"

"Mayhap they be not evil, but good, these spirits," others said. "It is known that his father was a mighty hunter. May not his father hunt with him so that he may attain excellence and patience and understanding? Who knows?"

Nonetheless, his success continued, and the less skillful hunters were often kept busy hauling in his meat. And in the division of it he was just. As his father had done before him, he saw to it that the least old woman and the least old man received a fair portion, keeping no more for himself than his needs required. And because of this, and of his merit as a hunter, he was looked upon with respect, and even awe; and there was talk of making him chief after old Klosh-Kwan. Because of the things he had done, they looked for him to appear again in the council, but he never came, and they were ashamed to ask.

"I am minded to build me an igloo," he said one day to Klosh-Kwan and a number of the hunters. "It shall be a large igloo, wherein Ikeega and I can dwell in comfort."

"Ay," they nodded gravely.

"But I have no time. My business is hunting,

and it takes all my time. So it is but just that the men and women of the village who eat my meat should build me my igloo."

And the igloo was built accordingly, on a generous scale which exceeded even the dwelling of Klosh-Kwan. Keesh and his mother moved into it, and it was the first prosperity she had enjoyed since the death of Bok. Nor was material prosperity alone hers, for because of her wonderful son and the position he had given her, she came to be looked upon as the first woman in all the village; and the women were given to visiting her, to asking her advice, and to quoting her wisdom when arguments arose among themselves or with the men.

But it was the mystery of Keesh's marvelous hunting that took chief place in all their minds. And one day Ugh-Gluk taxed him with witchcraft to his face.

"It is charged," Ugh-Gluk said ominously, "that thou dealest with evil spirits, wherefore thy hunting is rewarded."

"Is not the meat good?" Keesh made answer. "Has one in the village yet to fall sick from the eating of it? How dost thou know that witchcraft be concerned? Or dost thou guess, in the dark, merely because of the envy that consumes thee?"

And Ugh-Gluk withdrew discomfited, the women laughing at him as he walked away. But in the council one night, after long deliberation, it was determined to put spies on his track when he went forth to hunt, so that his methods might be learned. So, on his next trip, Bim and Bawn, two young men, and of hunters the craftiest, followed after him, taking care not to be seen. After five days they returned, their eyes bulging and their tongues atremble to tell what they had seen. The council was hastily called in Klosh-Kwan's dwelling, and Bim took up the tale.

"Brothers! As commanded, we journeyed on the trail of Keesh, and cunningly we journeyed, so that he might not know. And midway of the first day he picked up with a great he-bear. It was a very great bear."

"None greater," Bawn corroborated, and went on himself. "Yet was the bear not inclined to fight, for he turned away and made off slowly over the ice. This we saw from the rocks of the shore, and the bear came toward us and after him came Keesh, very much unafraid. And he shouted harsh words after the bear, and waved his arms about, and made much noise. Then did the bear grow angry, and rise up on his hind legs, and growl. But Keesh walked right up to the bear."

"Ay," Bim continued the story. "Right up to the bear Keesh walked. And the bear took after him, and Keesh ran away. But as he ran he dropped a little round ball on the ice. And the bear stopped and smelled of it, and then swallowed it up. And Keesh continued to run away and drop little round balls, and the bear continued to swallow them up."

Exclamations and cries of doubt were being made, and Ugh-Gluk expressed open unbelief.

"With our own eyes we saw it," Bim affirmed.

And Bawn — "Ay, with our own eyes. And this continued until the bear stood suddenly upright and cried aloud in pain, and thrashed his forepaws madly about. And Keesh continued to make off over the ice to a safe distance. But the bear gave him no notice, being occupied with the misfortune the little round balls had wrought within him."

"Ay, within him," Bim interrupted. "For he did claw at himself, and leap about over the ice like a playful puppy, save from the way he growled and squealed it was plain it was not play but pain. Never did I see such a sight!"

"Nay, never was such a sight seen," Bawn took up the strain. "And furthermore, it was such a large bear."

"Witchcraft," Ugh-Gluk suggested.

"I know not," Bawn replied. "I tell only of what my eyes beheld. And after a while the bear grew weak and tired, for he was very heavy and he had jumped about with exceeding violence, and he went off along the shore ice, shaking his head

33

slowly from side to side and sitting down ever and again to squeal and cry. And Keesh followed after the bear, and we followed after Keesh, and for that day and three days more we followed. The bear grew weak, and never ceased crying from his pain."

"It was a charm!" Ugh-Gluk exclaimed. "Surely it was a charm!"

"It may well be."

And Bim relieved Bawn. "The bear wandered, now this way and now that, doubling back and forth and crossing his trail in circles, so that at the end he was near where Keesh had first come upon him. By this time he was quite sick, the bear, and could crawl no farther, so Keesh came up close and speared him to death."

"And then?" Klosh-Kwan demanded.

"Then we left Keesh skinning the bear, and came running that the news of the killing might be told."

And in the afternoon of that day the women hauled in the meat of the bear while the men sat in council assembled. When Keesh arrived a messenger was sent to him, bidding him come to the council. But he sent reply, saying that he was hungry and tired; also that his igloo was large and comfortable and could hold many men.

And curiosity was so strong in the men that the whole council, Klosh-Kwan to the fore, rose up and went to the igloo of Keesh. He was eating, but he received them with respect and seated them according to their rank. Ikeega was proud and embarrassed by turns, but Keesh was quite composed.

Klosh-Kwan recited the information brought by Bim and Bawn, and at its close said in a stern voice: "So explanation is wanted, O Keesh, of thy manner of hunting. Is there witchcraft in it?"

Keesh looked up and smiled. "Nay, O Klosh-Kwan. It is not for a boy to know aught of witches, and of witches I know nothing. I have but devised a means whereby I may kill the ice bear with ease, that is all. It be headcraft, not witchcraft."

"And may any man?"

"Any man."

There was a long silence. The men looked in one another's faces, and Keesh went on eating.

"And . . . and . . . and wilt thou tell us, O Keesh?" Klosh-Kwan finally asked in a tremulous voice.

"Yea, I will tell thee." Keesh finished sucking a marrow-bone and rose to his feet. "It is quite simple. Behold!"

He picked up a thin strip of whalebone and showed it to them. The ends were sharp as needlepoints. The strip he coiled carefully, till it disappeared in his hand. Then, suddenly releasing

35

it, it sprang straight again. He picked up a piece of blubber.

"So," he said, "one takes a small chunk of blubber, thus, and thus makes it hollow. Then into the hollow goes the whalebone, so, tightly coiled, and another piece of blubber is fitted over the whalebone. After that it is put outside where it freezes into a little round ball. The bear swallows the little round ball, the blubber melts, the whalebone with its sharp ends stands out straight, the bear gets sick, and when the bear is very sick, why you kill him with a spear. It is quite simple."

And Ugh-Gluk said "Oh!" and Klosh-Kwan said "Ah!" And each said something after his own manner, and all understood.

And this is the story of Keesh, who lived long ago on the rim of the polar sea. Because he exercised headcraft and not witchcraft, he rose from the meanest igloo to be head man of his village, and through all the years that he lived, it is related, his tribe was prosperous, and neither widow nor weak one cried aloud in the night because there was no meat.

THE SUNDOG
TRAIL

3

SITKA CHARLEY smoked his pipe and gazed thoughtfully at the *Police Gazette* illustration on the wall. For half an hour he had been steadily regarding it, and for half an hour I had been slyly watching him. Something was going on in that mind of his, and whatever it was, I knew it was well worth knowing. He had lived life, and seen things, and performed that prodigy of prodigies, namely, the turning of his back upon his own people, and insofar as it was possible for an Indian, becoming a white man even in his mental processes. As he phrased it himself, he had come into the warm, sat among us by our fires, and become one of us. He had never learned to read or write, but his vocabulary was remarkable, and more remarkable still was the completeness with which he had assumed the white man's point of view, the white man's attitude toward things.

We had struck this deserted cabin after a hard day on trail. The dogs had been fed, the supper dishes washed, the beds made, and we were now enjoying that most delicious hour that comes each day — and but once each day — on the Alaskan trail, the hour when nothing intervenes between the tired body and bed save the smoking of the evening pipe. Some former denizen of the cabin had decorated its walls with illustrations torn from magazines and newspapers, and it was these illustrations that had held Sitka Charley's attention from the moment of our arrival two hours before. He had studied them intently, ranging from one to another and back again, and I could see that there was uncertainty in his mind, and puzzlement.

"Well?" I finally broke the silence.

He took the pipe from his mouth and said simply, "I do not understand."

He smoked on again, and again removed the pipe, using it to point at the *Police Gazette* illustration.

"That picture — what does it mean? I do not understand."

I looked at the picture. A man, with a preposterously wicked face, his right hand pressed dramatically to his heart, was falling backward to the floor. Confronting him, with a face that was a composite of destroying angel and Adonis, was a man holding a smoking revolver.

"One man is killing the other man," I said, aware of a distinct puzzlement of my own and of failure to explain.

"Why?" asked Sitka Charley.

"I do not know," I confessed.

"That picture is all end," he said. "It has no beginning."

"It is life," I said.

"Life has beginning," he objected.

I was silenced for the moment, while his eyes wandered on to an adjoining decoration, a photographic reproduction of somebody's "Leda and the Swan."

"That picture," he said, "has no beginning. It has no end. I do not understand pictures."

"Look at that picture," I commanded, pointing to a third decoration. "It means something. Tell me what it means to you."

He studied it for several minutes.

"The little girl is sick," he said finally. "That is the doctor looking at her. They have been up all night — see, the oil is low in the lamp, the first

39

morning light is coming in at the window. It is a great sickness; maybe she will die, that is why the doctor looks so hard. That is the mother. It is a great sickness, because the mother's head is on the table and she is crying."

"How do you know she is crying?" I interrupted. "You cannot see her face. Perhaps she is asleep."

Sitka Charley looked at me in swift surprise, then back at the picture. It was evident that he had not reasoned the impression.

"Perhaps she is asleep," he repeated. He studied it closely. "No, she is not asleep. The shoulders show that she is not asleep. I have seen the shoulders of a woman who cried. The mother is crying. It is a very great sickness."

"And now you understand the picture," I cried.

He shook his head, and asked, "The little girl — does it die?"

It was my turn for silence.

"Does it die?" he reiterated. "You are a painter-man. Maybe you know."

"No, I do not know," I confessed.

"It is not life," he delivered himself dogmatically. "In life little girl die or get well. Something happen in life. In picture nothing happen. No, I do not understand pictures."

His disappointment was patent. It was his desire to understand all things that white men understand,

The Sundog Trail

and here, in this matter, he failed. I felt, also, that there was challenge in his attitude. He was bent upon compelling me to show him the wisdom of pictures. Besides, he had remarkable powers of visualization. I had long since learned this. He visualized everything. He saw life in pictures, felt life in pictures, generalized life in pictures; and yet he did not understand pictures when seen through other men's eyes and expressed by those men with color and line upon canvas.

"Pictures are bits of life," I said. "We paint life as we see it. For instance, Charley, you are coming along the trail. It is night. You see a cabin. The window is lighted. You look through the window for one second, or for two seconds, you see something, and you go on your way. You saw maybe a man writing a letter. You saw something without beginning or end. Nothing happened. Yet it was a bit of life you saw. You remember it afterward. It is like a picture in your memory. The window is the frame of the picture."

I could see that he was interested, and I knew that as I spoke he had looked through the window and seen the man writing the letter.

"There is a picture you have painted that I understand," he said. "It is a true picture. It has much meaning. It is in your cabin at Dawson. It

41

is a faro table. There are men playing. It is a large game. The limit is off."

"How do you know the limit is off?" I broke in excitedly, for here was where my work could be tried out on an unbiased judge who knew life only, and not art, and who was a sheer master of reality. Also, I was very proud of that particular piece of work. I had named it "The Last Turn," and I believed it to be one of the best things I had ever done.

"There are no chips on the table," Sitka Charley explained. "The men are playing with markers. That means the roof is the limit. One man play yellow markers — maybe one yellow marker worth one thousand dollars, maybe two thousand dollars. One man play red markers. Maybe they are worth five hundred dollars, maybe one thousand dollars. It is a very big game. Everybody play very high, up to the roof. How do I know? You make the dealer with blood little bit warm in face." (I was delighted.) "The lookout, you make him lean forward in his chair. Why he lean forward? Why his face very much quiet? Why his eyes very much bright? Why dealer warm with blood a little bit in the face? Why all men very quiet? — the man with yellow markers? the man with white markers? the man with red markers? Why nobody talk? Because very much money. Because last turn."

"How do you know it is the last turn?" I asked.

"The king is coppered, the seven is played open," he answered. "Nobody bet on other cards. Other cards all gone. Everybody one mind. Everybody play king to lose, seven to win. Maybe bank lose twenty thousand dollars, maybe bank win. Yes, that picture I understand."

"Yet you do not know the end!" I cried triumphantly. "It is the last turn, but the cards are not yet turned. In the picture they will never be turned. Nobody will ever know who wins nor who loses."

"And the men will sit there and never talk," he said, wonder and awe growing in his face. "And the lookout will lean forward, and the blood will be warm in the face of the dealer. It is a strange thing. Always will they sit there, always; and the cards will never be turned."

"It is a picture," I said. "It is life. You have seen things like it yourself."

He looked at me and pondered, then said, very slowly: "No, as you say, there is no end to it. Nobody will ever know the end. Yet it is a true thing. I have seen it. It is life."

For a long time he smoked on in silence, weighing the pictorial wisdom of the white man and verifying it by the facts of life. He nodded his head several times, and grunted once or twice. Then he knocked the ashes from his pipe, carefully refilled it, and, after a thoughtful pause, lighted it again.

"Then have I, too, seen many pictures of life," he began; "pictures not painted, but seen with the eyes. I have looked at them like through the window at the man writing the letter. I have seen many pieces of life, without beginning, without end, without understanding."

With a sudden change of position he turned his eyes full upon me and regarded me thoughtfully.

"Look you," he said; "You are a painter-man. How would you paint this which I saw, a picture without beginning, the ending of which I do not understand, a piece of life with the northern lights for a candle and Alaska for a frame."

"It is a large canvas," I murmured.

But he ignored me, for the picture he had in mind was before his eyes and he was seeing it.

"There are many names for this picture," he said. "But in the picture there are many sundogs, and it comes into my mind to call it 'The Sundog Trail.' It was a long time ago, seven years ago, the fall of '97, when I saw the woman first time. At Lake Linderman I had one canoe, very good Peterborough canoe. I came over Chilcoot Pass with two thousand letters for Dawson. I was letter carrier. Everybody rush to Klondike at that time. Many people on trail. Many people chop down trees and make boats. Last water, snow in the air, snow on the ground, ice on the lake, on the river ice in the eddies. Every day more snow, more ice. Maybe one day, maybe three days, maybe six days, any day maybe freeze-up come, then no more water, all ice, everybody walk. Dawson six hundred miles, long time walk. Boat go very quick. Everybody want to go boat. Everybody say, 'Charley, two hundred dollars you take me in canoe,' 'Charley, three hundred dollars,' 'Charley, four hundred dollars.' I say no, all the time I say no. I am letter carrier.

"In morning I get to Lake Linderman. I walk all night and am much tired. I cook breakfast, I eat, then I sleep on the beach three hours. I wake up. It is ten o'clock. Snow is falling. There is wind, much wind that blows fair. Also, there is a woman who sits in the snow alongside. She is white woman, she is young, very pretty, maybe she is twenty years old, maybe twenty-five years old. She look at me. I look at her. She is very tired. She is no dance-woman. I see that right away. She is good woman, and she is very tired.

" 'You are Sitka Charley,' she says. I get up quick and roll blankets so snow does not get inside. 'I go to Dawson,' she says. 'I go in your canoe — how much?'

"I do not want anybody in my canoe. I do not

like to say no. So I say, 'One thousand dollars.' Just for fun I say it, so woman cannot come with me, much better than say no. She look at me very hard, then she says, 'When you start?' I say right away. Then she says all right, she will give me one thousand dollars.

"What can I say? I do not want the woman, yet have I given my word that for one thousand dollars she can come. I am surprised. Maybe she make fun, too, so I say, 'Let me see thousand dollars.' And that woman, that young woman, all alone on the trail, there in the snow, she take out one thousand dollars, in greenbacks, and she put them in my hand. I look at money, I look at her. What can I say? I say, 'No, my canoe very small. There is no room for outfit.' She laugh. She says, 'I am great traveler. This is my outfit,' She kick one small pack in the snow. It is two fur robes, canvas outside, some woman's clothes inside. I pick it up. Maybe thirty-five pounds. I am surprised. She take it away from me. She says, 'Come, let us start,' She carries pack into canoe. What can I say? I put my blankets into canoe. We start.

"And that is the way I saw the woman first time. The wind was fair. I put up small sail. The canoe went very fast, it flew like a bird over the high waves. The woman was much afraid. 'What for you come Klondike much afraid?' I ask. She laugh at me, a hard laugh, but she is still much afraid. Also is she very tired. I run canoe through rapids to Lake Bennett. Water very bad, and woman cry out because she is afraid. We go down Lake Bennett, snow, ice, wind like a gale, but woman is very tired and go to sleep.

"That night we make camp at Windy Arm. Woman sit by fire and eat supper. I look at her. She is pretty. She fix hair. There is much hair, and it is brown, also sometimes it is like gold in the firelight, when she turn her head, so, and flashes come from it like golden fire. The eyes are large and brown, sometimes warm like a candle behind a curtain, sometimes very hard and bright like broken ice when sun shines upon it. When she smile — how can I say? — when she smile I know white man like to kiss her, just like that, when she smile. She never do hard work. Her hands are soft, like baby's hand. She is soft all over, like baby. She is not thin, but round like baby; her arm, her leg, her muscles, all soft and round like baby. Her waist is small, and when she stand up, when she walk, or move her head or arm, it is — I do not know the word — but it is nice to look at, like — maybe I say she is built on lines like the lines of a good canoe, just like that, and when she move she is like the movement of the good canoe sliding through still water or leaping through

47

water when it is white and fast and angry. It is very good to see.

"Why does she come into Klondike, all alone, with plenty of money? I do not know. Next day I ask her. She laugh and says: 'Sitka Charley, that is none of your business. I give you one thousand dollars take me to Dawson. That only is your business.' Next day after that I ask her what is her name. She laugh, then she says, 'Mary Jones, that is my name.' I do not know her name, but I know all the time that Mary Jones is not her name.

"It is very cold in canoe, and because of cold sometimes she not feel good. Sometimes she feel good and she sing. Her voice is like a silver bell, and I feel good all over like when I go into church at Holy Cross Mission, and when she sing I feel strong and paddle like hell. Then she laugh and says, 'You think we get to Dawson before freeze-up, Charley?' Sometimes she sit in canoe and is thinking far away, her eyes like that, all empty. She does not see Sitka Charley, nor the ice, nor the snow. She is far away. Very often she is like that, thinking far away. Sometimes, when she is thinking far away, her face is not good to see. It looks like a face that is angry, like the face of one man when he want to kill another man.

"Last day to Dawson very bad. Shore ice in all the eddies, mush ice in the stream. I cannot paddle. The canoe freeze to ice. I cannot get to shore. There is much danger. All the time we go down Yukon in the ice. That night there is much noise of ice. Then ice stop, canoe stop, everything stop. 'Let us go to shore,' the woman says. I say no, better wait. By and by, everything start downstream again. There is much snow. I cannot see. At eleven o'clock at night, everything stop. At one o'clock everything start again. At three o'clock everything stop. Canoe is smashed like eggshell, but is on top of ice and cannot sink. I hear dogs howling. We wait. We sleep. By-and-by morning come. There is no more snow. It is the freeze-up, and there is Dawson. Canoe smash and stop right at Dawson. Sitka Charley has come in with two thousand letters on very last water.

"The woman rent a cabin on the hill, and for one week I see her no more. Then, one day she come to me. 'Charley,' she says, 'how do you like to work for me? You drive dogs, make camp, travel with me.' I say that I make too much money carrying letters. She says 'Charley, I will pay you more money.' I tell her that pick-and-shovel man get fifteen dollars a day in the mines. She says, 'That is four hundred and fifty dollars a month.' And I say, 'Sitka Charley is no pick-and-shovel man.' Then she says, 'I understand, Charley. I will give you seven hundred and fifty dollars each month.'

It is a good price, and I go to work for her. I buy for her dogs and sled. We travel up Klondike, up Bonanza and Eldorado, over to Indian River, to Sulphur Creek, to Dominion, back across divide to Gold Bottom and to Too Much Gold, and back to Dawson. All the time she look for something, I do not know what. I am puzzled. 'What thing you look for?' I ask. She laugh. 'You look for gold?' I ask. She laugh. Then she says, 'That is none of your business, Charley.' And after that I never ask any more.

"She has a small revolver which she carries in her belt. Sometimes, on trail, she makes practice with revolver. I laugh. 'What for you laugh, Charley?' she ask. 'What for you play with that?' I say. 'It is no good. It is too small. It is for a child, a little plaything.' When we get back to Dawson she ask me to buy good revolver for her. I buy a Colt's 44. It is very heavy, but she carry it in her belt all the time.

"At Dawson comes the man. Which way he come I do not know. Only do I know he is *che-cha-quo* —what you call tenderfoot. His hands are soft, just like hers. He never do hard work. He is soft all over. At first I think maybe he is her husband. But he is too young. He is maybe twenty years old. His eyes blue, his hair yellow, he has a little mustache which is yellow. His name is John Jones.

Maybe he is her brother. I do not know. I ask
questions no more. Only I think his name not
John Jones. Other people call him Mr. Girvan.
I do not think that is his name. I do not think her
name is Miss Girvan, which other people call her.
I think nobody know their names.

"One night I am asleep at Dawson. He wake
me up. He says, 'Get the dogs ready; we start.'
No more do I ask questions, so I get the dogs ready
and we start. We go down the Yukon. It is nighttime, it is November, and it is very cold — sixty-
five below. She is soft. He is soft. The cold bites.
They get tired. They cry under their breath to
themselves. By-and-by I say better we stop and
make camp. But they say that they will go on.
Three times I say better to make camp and rest,
but each time they say they will go on. After that
I say nothing. All the time, day after day, is it that
way. They are very soft. They get stiff and sore.
They do not understand moccasins, and their feet
hurt very much. They limp, they stagger like
drunken people, they cry under their breath; and all
the time they say, 'On! on! We will go on!'

"They are like crazy people. All the time do
they go on, and on. Why do they go on? I do not
know. Only do they go on. What are they after?
I do not know. They are not after gold. There is no
stampede. Besides, they spend plenty of money.

But I ask questions no more. I, too, go on and on, because I am strong on the trail and because I am greatly paid.

"We make Circle City. That for which they look is not there. I think now that we will rest, and rest the dogs. But we do not rest, not for one day do we rest. 'Come,' says the woman to the man, 'let us go on.' And we go on. We leave the Yukon. We cross the divide to the west and swing down into the Tanana country. There are new diggings there. But that for which they look is not there, and we take the back trail to Circle City.

"It is a hard journey. December is most gone. The days are short. It is very cold. One morning it is seventy below zero. 'Better that we do not travel today,' I say, 'else will the frost be unwarmed in the breathing and bite all the edges of our lungs. After that we will have bad cough, and maybe next spring will come pneumonia.' But they are *che-cha-quo*. They do not understand the trail. They are like dead people they are so tired, but they say, 'Let us go on.' We go on. The frost bites their lungs, and they get the dry cough. They cough till the tears run down their cheeks. When bacon is frying they must run away from the fire and cough half an hour in the snow. They freeze their cheeks a little bit, so that the skin turns black and is very sore. Also, the man freezes his thumb till the end is like to come off, and he must wear a large mitten on his thumb to keep it warm. And sometimes, when the frost bites hard and the thumb is very cold, he must take off the mitten and put the hand between his legs next to the skin, so that the thumb may get warm again.

"We limp into Circle City, and even I, Sitka Charley, am tired. It is Christmas Eve. I dance, drink, make a good time, for tomorrow is Christmas Day and we will rest. But no. It is five o'clock in the morning — Christmas morning. I am two hours asleep. The man stand by my bed. 'Come, Charley,' he says, 'harness the dogs. We start.'

"Have I not said that I ask questions no more? They pay me seven hundred and fifty dollars each month. They are my masters. I am their man. If they say, 'Charley, come, let us start for hell,' I will harness the dogs, and snap the whip, and start for hell. So I harness the dogs, and we start down the Yukon. Where do we go? They do not say. Only do they say. 'On! on! We will go on!'

"They are very weary. They have traveled many hundreds of miles, and they do not understand the way of the trail. Besides, their cough is very bad — the dry cough that makes strong men swear and weak men cry. But they go on. Every day they go on. Never do they rest the dogs. Always do they buy new dogs. At every camp, at every post, at every Indian village, do they cut out the tired dogs and put in fresh dogs. They have much money, money without end, and like water they spend it. They are crazy? Sometimes I think so, for there is a devil in them that drives them on and on, always on. What is it that they try to find? It is not gold. Never do they dig in the ground. I think a long time. Then I think it is a man they try to find. But what man? Never do we see the man. Yet are they like wolves on the trail of the kill. But they are funny wolves, soft wolves, baby wolves who do not understand the way of the trail. They cry aloud in their sleep at night. In their sleep they moan and groan with the pain of their weariness. And in the day, as they stagger along the trail, they cry under their breath. They are funny wolves.

"We pass Fort Yukon. We pass Fort Hamilton. We pass Minook. January has come and nearly gone. The days are very short. At nine o'clock comes daylight. At three o'clock comes night. And it is cold. And even I, Sitka Charley, am tired. Will we go on forever this way without end? I do not know. But always do I look along the trail for that which they try to find. There are few people on the trail. Sometimes we travel one hundred miles and never see a sign of life. It is very quiet. There is no sound. Sometimes it snows, and we are like wandering ghosts. Sometimes it is clear and at midday the sun looks at us for a moment over the hills to the south. The northern lights flame in the sky, and the sundogs dance, and the air is filled with frost dust.

"I am Sitka Charley, a strong man. I was born on the trail, and all my days have I lived on the trail. And yet have these two baby wolves made me very tired. I am lean, like a starved cat, and I am glad of my bed at night, and in the morning am I greatly weary. Yet ever are we hitting the trail in the dark before daylight, and still on the trail does the dark after nightfall find us. These two baby wolves! If I am lean like a starved cat, they are lean like cats that have never eaten and have died. Their eyes are sunk deep in their heads, bright sometimes as with fever, dim and cloudy sometimes like the eyes of the dead. Their cheeks are hollow like caves in a cliff. Also are their cheeks black and raw from many freezings. Sometimes it is the woman in the morning who says, 'I cannot get up. I cannot move. Let me die.' And it is the man who stands beside her and says, 'Come, let us go on.' And they go on. And sometimes it is the man who cannot get up, and the woman says, 'Come, let us go on.' But the one thing they do, and always do, is to go on. Always do they go on.

"Sometimes, at the trading posts, the man and woman get letters. I do not know what is in the

55

letters. But it is the scent that they follow, these letters themselves are the scent. One time an Indian gives them a letter. I talk with him privately. He says it is a man with one eye who gives him the letter, a man who travels fast down the Yukon. That is all. But I know that the baby wolves are after the man with the one eye.

"It is February, and we have traveled fifteen hundred miles. We are getting near Bering Sea, and there are storms and blizzards. The going is hard. We come to Anvig. I do not know, but I think sure they get a letter at Anvig, for they are much excited, and they say, 'Come, hurry, let us go on.' But I say we must buy grub, and they say we must travel light and fast. Also, they say that we can get grub at Charley McKeon's cabin. Then do I know that they take the big cutoff, for it is there that Charley McKeon lives where the Black Rock stands by the trail.

"Before we start, I talk maybe two minutes with the priest at Anvig. Yes, there is a man with one eye who has gone by and who travels fast. And I know that for which they look is the man with the one eye. We leave Anvig with little grub, and travel light and fast. There are three fresh dogs bought in Anvig, and we travel very fast. The man and woman are like mad. We start earlier in the morning, we travel later at night. I look sometimes

to see them die, these two baby wolves, but they
will not die. They go on and on. When the dry
cough take hold of them hard, they hold up their
hands against their stomach and double up in the
snow, and cough, and cough, and cough. They
cannot walk, they cannot talk. Maybe for ten minutes they cough, maybe for half an hour, and then
they straighten up, the tears from the coughing
frozen on their faces, and the words they say are,
'Come, let us go on.'

"Even I, Sitka Charley, am greatly weary, and
I think seven hundred and fifty dollars is a cheap
price for the labor I do. We take the big cutoff,
and the trail is fresh. The baby wolves have their
noses down to the trail, and they say, 'Hurry!' All
the time do they say, 'Hurry! Faster! Faster!' It is
hard on the dogs. We have not much food and
we cannot give them enough to eat, and they grow
weak. Also, they must work hard. The woman has
true sorrow for them, and often, because of them,
the tears are in her eyes. But the devil in her that
drives her on will not let her stop and rest the dogs.

"And then we come upon the man with the one
eye. He is in the snow by the trail, and his leg is
broken. Because of the leg he has made a poor
camp, and has been lying on his blankets for three
days and keeping a fire going. When we find him
he is swearing. Never have I heard a man swear

57

like that man. I am glad. Now that they have found that for which they look, we will have rest. But the woman says, 'Let us start. Hurry!'

"I am surprised. But the man with the one eye says, 'Never mind me. Give me your grub. You will get more grub at McKeon's cabin tomorrow. Send McKeon back for me. But do you go on.' Here is another wolf, an old wolf, and he, too, thinks but the one thought, to go on. So we give him our grub, which is not much, and we chop wood for his fire, and we take his strongest dogs and go on. We left the man with one eye there in the snow, and he died there in the snow, for McKeon never went back for him. And who that man was, and why he came to be there, I do not know. But I think he was greatly paid by the man and the woman, like me, to do their work for them.

"That day and that night we had nothing to eat, and all next day we traveled fast, and we were weak with hunger. Then we came to the Black Rock, which rose five hundred feet above the trail. It was at the end of the day. Darkness was coming, and we could not find the cabin of McKeon. We slept hungry, and in the morning looked for the cabin. It was not there, which was a strange thing, for everybody knew that McKeon lived in a cabin at Black Rock. We were near to the coast, where the wind blows hard and there is much snow.

Everywhere there were small hills of snow where the wind had piled it up. I have a thought, and I dig in one and another of the hills of snow. Soon I find the walls of the cabin, and I dig down to the door. I go inside. McKeon is dead. Maybe two or three weeks he is dead. A sickness had come upon him so that he could not leave the cabin. The wind and the snow had covered the cabin. He had eaten his grub and died. I looked for his cache, but there was no grub in it.

"'Let us go on,' said the woman. Her eyes were hungry, and her hand was upon her heart, as with the hurt of something inside. She bent back and forth like a tree in the wind as she stood there. 'Yes, let us go on,' said the man. His voice was hollow, like the *klonk* of an old raven, and he was hunger-mad. His eyes were like live coals of fire, and as his body rocked to and fro, so rocked his soul inside. And I, too, said, 'Let us go on.' For that one thought, laid upon me like a lash for every mile of fifteen hundred miles, had burned itself into my soul, and I think that I, too, was mad. Besides, we could only go on, for there was no grub. And we went on, giving no thought to the man with the one eye in the snow.

"There is little travel on the big cutoff. Sometimes two or three months and nobody goes by. The snow had covered the trail, and there was no sign that men had ever come or gone that way. All day the wind blew and the snow fell, and all day we traveled, while our stomachs gnawed their desire and our bodies grew weaker with every step they took. Then the woman began to fall. Then the man. I did not fall, but my feet were heavy and I caught my toes and stumbled many times.

"That night is the end of February. I kill three ptarmigan with the woman's revolver, and we are made somewhat strong again. But the dogs have nothing to eat. They try to eat their harness, which is of leather and walrus hide, and I must fight them off with a club and hang all the harness in a tree. And all night they howl and fight around that tree. But we do not mind. We sleep like dead people, and in the morning get up like dead people out of their graves and go on along the trail.

"That morning is the first of March, and on that morning I see the first sign of that after which the baby wolves are in search. It is clear weather, and cold. The sun stay longer in the sky, and there are sundogs flashing on either side, and the air is bright with frost dust. The snow falls no more upon the trail, and I see the fresh sign of dogs and sled. There is one man with that outfit, and I see in the snow that he is not strong. He, too, has not enough to eat. The young wolves see the fresh sign, too, and they are much excited. 'Hurry!' they say. All the time they say, 'Hurry! Faster, Charley, faster!'

"We make hurry very slow. All the time the man and the woman fall down. When they try to ride on sled the dogs are too weak, and the dogs fall down. Besides, it is so cold that if they ride on the sled they will freeze. It is very easy for a hungry man to freeze. When the woman fall down, the man help her up. Sometimes the woman help the man up. By-and-by both fall down and cannot get up, and I must help them up all the time, else they will not get up and will die there in the snow. This is very hard work, for I am greatly weary, and as well I must drive the dogs, and the man and woman are very heavy with no strength in their bodies. So by-and-by, I, too, fall down in the snow, and there is no one to help me up. I must get up by myself. And always do I get up by myself, and help them up, and make the dogs go on.

"That night I get one ptarmigan, and we are very hungry. And that night the man says to me, 'What time start tomorrow, Charley?' It is like the voice of a ghost. I say, 'All the time you make start at five o'clock.' 'Tomorrow,' he says, 'we will start at three o'clock.' I laugh in great bitterness, and I say, 'You are dead man.' And he says, 'Tomorrow we will start at three o'clock.'

"And we start at three o'clock, for I am their

man, and that which they say is to be done, I do. It is clear and cold, and there is no wind. When daylight comes we can see a long way off. And it is very quiet. We can hear no sound but the beat of our hearts, and in the silence that is a very loud sound. We are like sleepwalkers, and we walk in dreams until we fall down; and then we know we must get up, and we see the trail once more and hear the beating of our hearts. Sometimes, when I am walking in dreams this way, I have strange thoughts. Why does Sitka Charley live? I ask myself. Why does Sitka Charley work hard, and go hungry, and have all this pain? For seven hundred and fifty dollars a month, I make the answer, and I know it is a foolish answer. Also it is a true answer. And after that never again do I care for money. For that day a large wisdom came to me. There was a great light, and I saw clear, and I knew that it was not for money that a man must live, but for a happiness that no man can give, or buy, or sell, and that is beyond all value of all money in the world.

"In the morning we come upon the last-night camp of the man who is before us. It is a poor camp, the kind a man makes who is hungry and without strength. On the snow there are pieces of blanket and of canvas, and I know what has happened. His dogs have eaten their harness, and he has made new harness out of his blankets. The man and woman stare hard at what is to be seen, and as I look at them my back feels the chill as of a cold wind against the skin. Their eyes are toil-mad and hunger-mad, and burn like fire deep in their heads. Their faces are like the faces of people who have died of hunger, and their cheeks are black with the dead flesh of many freezings. 'Let us go on,' says the man. But the woman coughs and falls in the snow. It is the dry cough where the frost has bitten the lungs. For a long time she coughs, then like a woman crawling out of her grave she crawls to her feet. The tears are ice upon her cheeks, and her breath makes a noise as it comes and goes, and she says, 'Let us go on.'

"We go on. And we walk in dreams through the silence. And every time we walk is a dream and we are without pain; and every time we fall down is an awakening, and we see the snow and the mountains and the fresh trail of the man who is before us, and we know all our pain again. We come to where we can see a long way over the snow, and that for which they look is before them. A mile away there are black spots upon the snow. The black spots move. My eyes are dim, and I must stiffen my soul to see. And I see one man with dogs and a sled. The baby wolves see, too.

They can no longer talk, but they whisper, 'On, on. Let us hurry!'

"And they fall down, but they go on. The man who is before us, his blanket harness breaks often, and he must stop and mend it. Our harness is good, for I have hung it in trees each night. At eleven o'clock the man is half a mile away. At one o'clock he is a quarter of a mile away. He is very weak. We see him fall down many times in the snow. One of his dogs can no longer travel, and he cuts it out of the harness. But he does not kill it. I kill it with the axe as I go by, as I kill one of my dogs which loses its legs and can travel no more.

"Now we are three hundred yards away. We go very slow. Maybe in two, three hours we go one mile. We do not walk. All the time we fall down. We stand up and stagger two steps, maybe three steps, then we fall down again. And all the time I must help up the man and woman. Sometimes they rise to their knees and fall forward, maybe four or five times before they can get to their feet again and stagger two or three steps and fall. But always do they fall forward. Standing or kneeling, always do they fall forward, gaining on the trail each time by the length of their bodies.

"Sometimes they crawl on hands and knees like animals that live in the forest. We go like snails, like snails that are dying we go so slow. And yet we go faster than the man who is before us. For he, too, falls all the time, and there is no Sitka Charley to lift him up. Now he is two hundred yards away. After a long time he is one hundred yards away.

"It is a funny sight. I want to laugh out loud, Ha! ha! just like that, it is so funny. It is a race of dead men and dead dogs. It is like in a dream when you have a nightmare and run away very fast for your life and go very slow. The man who is with me is mad. The woman is mad. I am mad. All the world is mad, and I want to laugh, it is so funny.

"The stranger-man who is before us leaves his dogs behind and goes on alone across the snow. After a long time we come to the dogs. They lie helpless in the snow, their harness of blanket and canvas on them, the sled behind them, and as we pass them they whine to us and cry like babies that are hungry.

"Then we, too, leave our dogs and go on alone across the snow. The man and the woman are nearly gone, and they moan and groan and sob, but they go on. I, too, go on. I have but one thought. It is to come up to the stranger-man. Then it is that I shall rest, and not until then shall

65

I rest, and it seem that I must lie down and sleep for a thousand years, I am so tired.

"The stranger-man is fifty yards away, all alone in the white snow. He falls and crawls, staggers, and falls and crawls again. He is like an animal that is sore wounded and trying to run from the hunter. By-and-by he crawls on hands and knees. He no longer stands up. And the man and woman no longer stand up. They, too, crawl after him on hands and knees. But I stand up. Sometimes I fall, but always do I stand up again.

"It is a strange thing to see. All about is the snow and the silence, and through it crawl the man and the woman, and the stranger-man who goes before. On either side the sun are sundogs, so that there are three suns in the sky. The frost dust is like the dust of diamonds, and all the air is filled with it. Now the woman coughs, and lies still in the snow until the fit has passed, when she crawls on again. Now the man looks ahead, and he is blear-eyed as with old age and must rub his eyes so that he can see the stranger-man. And now the stranger-man looks back over his shoulder. And Sitka Charley, standing upright, maybe falls down and stands upright again.

"After a long time the stranger-man crawls no more. He stands slowly upon his feet and rocks back and forth. Also does he take off one mitten and wait with revolver in his hand, rocking back and forth as he waits. His face is skin and bones and frozen black. It is a hungry face. The eyes are deep-sunk in his head, and the lips are snarling. The man and woman, too, get upon their feet and they go toward him very slowly. And all about is the snow and the silence. And in the sky are three suns, and all the air is flashing with the dust of diamonds.

"And thus it was that I, Sitka Charley, saw the baby wolves make their kill. No word is spoken. Only does the stranger-man snarl with his hungry face. Also does he rock to and fro, his shoulders drooping, his knees bent, and his legs wide apart so that he does not fall down. The man and the woman stop maybe fifty feet away. Their legs, too, are wide apart so that they do not fall down, and their bodies rock to and fro. The stranger-man is very weak. His arm shakes, so that when he shoots at the man his bullet strikes in the snow. The man cannot take off his mitten. The stranger-man shoots at him again, and this time the bullet goes by in the air. Then the man takes the mitten in his teeth and pulls it off. But his hand is frozen and he cannot hold the revolver, and it falls in the snow. I look at the woman. Her mitten is off, and the big Colt's revolver is in her hand. Three times she shoot, quick, just like that. The hungry

67

face of the stranger-man is still snarling as he falls forward into the snow.

"They do not look at the dead man. 'Let us go on,' they say. And we go on. But now that they have found that for which they look, they are like dead. The last strength has gone out of them. They can stand no more upon their feet. They will not crawl, but desire only to close their eyes and sleep. I see not far away a place for camp. I kick them. I have my dog whip, and I give them the lash of it. They cry aloud, but they must crawl. And they do crawl to the place for camp. I build fire so that they will not freeze. Then I go back for sled. Also, I kill the dogs of the stranger-man so that we may have food and not die. I put the man and woman in blankets and they sleep. Sometimes I wake them and give them little bit of food. They are not awake, but they take the food. The woman sleep one day and a half. Then she wake up and go to sleep again. The man sleep two days and wake up and go to sleep again. After that we go down to the coast at St. Michaels. And when the ice goes out of Bering Sea, the man and woman go away on a steamship. But first they pay me my seven hundred and fifty dollars a month. Also, they make me a present of one thousand dollars. And that was the year that Sitka Charley gave much money to the Mission at Holy Cross."

"But why did they kill the man?" I asked.

Sitka Charley delayed reply until he had lighted his pipe. He glanced at the *Police Gazette* illustration and nodded his head at it familiarly. Then he said, speaking slowly and ponderingly:

"I have thought much. I do not know. It is something that happened. It is a picture I remember. It is like looking in at the window and seeing the man writing a letter. They came into my life and they went out of my life, and the picture is as I have said, without beginning, the end without understanding."

"You have painted many pictures in the telling," I said.

"Ay," he nodded his head. "But they were without beginning and without end."

"The last picture of all had an end." I said.

"Ay," he answered. "But what end?"

"It was a piece of life." I said.

"Ay," he answered. "It was a piece of life."

NAM-BOK THE
UNVERACIOUS

4

"**A**BIDARKA, is it not so? Look! a bidarka,
and one man who drives clumsily with a
paddle!"

Old Bask-Wah-Wan rose to her knees, trembling with weakness and eagerness, and gazed
out over the sea.

"Nam-Bok was ever clumsy at the paddle," she
maundered reminiscently, shading the sun from
her eyes and staring across the silver-spilled water.
"Nam-Bok was ever clumsy. I remember . . ."

But the women and children laughed loudly,
and there was a gentle mockery in their laugh-

ter, and her voice dwindled till her lips moved
without sound.

Koogah lifted his grizzled head from his bone-
carving and followed the path of her eyes. Ex-
cept when wide yaws took it off its course, a bidarka
was heading in for the beach. Its occupant was
paddling with more strength than dexterity, and
made his approach along the zigzag line of most
resistance. Koogah's head dropped to his work
again, and on the ivory tusk between his knees
he scratched the dorsal fin of a fish the like of
which never swam in the sea.

"It is doubtless the man from the next village,"
he said finally, "come to consult with me about
the marking of things on bone. And the man is a
clumsy man. He will never know how."

"It is Nam-Bok," old Bask-Wah-Wan repeated.
"Should I not know my son?" she demanded shrilly.
"I say, and I say again, it is Nam-Bok."

"And so thou hast said these many summers,"
one of the women chided softly. "Ever when the
ice passed out of the sea hast thou sat and watched
through the long day, saying at each chance canoe,
'This is Nam-Bok.' Nam-Bok is dead, O Bask-Wah-
Wan, and the dead do not come back. It cannot be
that the dead come back."

"Nam-Bok!" the old woman cried, so loud and

clear that the whole village was startled and looked at her.

She struggled to her feet and tottered down the sand. She stumbled over a baby lying in the sun, and the mother hushed its crying and hurled harsh words after the old woman, who took no notice. The children ran down the beach in advance of her, and as the man in the bidarka drew closer, nearly capsizing with one of his ill-directed strokes, the women followed. Koogah dropped his walrus tusk and went also, leaning heavily upon his staff, and after him loitered the men in twos and threes.

The bidarka turned broadside and the ripple of surf threatened to swamp it, only a naked boy ran into the water and pulled the bow high up on the sand. The man stood up and sent a questing glance along the line of villagers. A rainbow sweater, dirty and the worse for wear, clung loosely to his broad shoulders, and a red cotton handkerchief was knotted in sailor fashion about his throat. A fisherman's tam-o'-shanter on his close-clipped head, and dungaree trousers and heavy brogans completed his outfit.

But he was nonetheless a striking personage to these simple fisherfolk of the great Yukon Delta, who, all their lives, had stared out on Bering Sea and in that time seen but two white men — the census enumerator and a lost Jesuit priest. They

were a poor people, with neither gold in the ground
nor valuable furs in hand, so the whites had passed
them afar. Also, the Yukon, through the thousands
of years, had shoaled that portion of the sea with
the detritus of Alaska till vessels grounded out of
sight of land. So the sodden coast, with its long
inside reaches and huge mudland archipelagoes,
was avoided by the ships of men, and the fisherfolk knew not that such things were.

Koogah, the Bone-Scratcher, retreated backward
in sudden haste, tripping over his staff and falling
to the ground. "Nam-Bok!" he cried, as he
scrambled wildly for footing. "Nam-Bok, who was
blown off to sea, come back!"

The men and women shrank away, and the
children scuttled off between their legs. Only
Opee-Kwan was brave, as befitted the head man
of the village. He strode forward and gazed long
and earnestly at the newcomer.

"It *is* Nam-Bok," he said at last, and at the
conviction in his voice the women wailed appre-
hensively and drew farther away.

The lips of the stranger moved indecisively, and
his brown throat writhed and wrestled with un-
spoken words.

"La, la, it is Nam-Bok," Bask-Wah-Wan croaked,
peering up into his face. "Ever did I say Nam-Bok
would come back."

73

"Ay, it is Nam-Bok come back." This time it was Nam-Bok himself who spoke, putting a leg over the side of the bidarka and standing with one foot afloat and one ashore. Again his throat writhed and wrestled as he grappled after forgotten words. And when the words came forth they were strange of sound and a spluttering of the lips accompanied the gutterals. "Greetings, O brothers," he said, "brothers of old time before I went away with the offshore wind."

He stepped out with both feet on the sand, and Opee-Kwan waved him back.

"Thou art dead, Nam-Bok," he said.

Nam-Bok laughed. "I am fat."

"Dead men are not fat," Opee-Kwan confessed. "Thou hast fared well, but it is strange. No man may mate with the offshore wind and come back on the heels of the years."

"I have come back," Nam-Bok answered simply.

"Mayhap thou art a shadow, then, a passing shadow of the Nam-Bok that was. Shadows come back."

"I am hungry. Shadows do not eat."

But Opee-Kwan doubted, and brushed his hand across his brow in sore puzzlement. Nam-Bok was likewise puzzled, and as he looked up and down the line found no welcome in the eyes of the fisherfolk. The men and women whispered to-

gether. The children stole timidly back among
their elders, and bristling dogs fawned up to him
and sniffed suspiciously.

"I bore thee, Nam-Bok, and I gave thee suck
when thou wast little," Bask-Wah-Wan whim-
pered, drawing closer; "and shadow though thou
be, or no shadow, I will give thee to eat now."

Nam-Bok made to come to her, but a growl of
fear and menace warned him back. He said something angrily in a strange tongue, and added, "No
shadow am I, but a man."

"Who may know concerning the things of mystery?" Opee-Kwan demanded, half of himself and
half of his tribespeople. "We are, and in a breath
we are not. If the man may become shadow, may
not the shadow become man? Nam-Bok was, but
is not. This we know, but we do not know if this
be Nam-Bok or the shadow of Nam-Bok."

Nam-Bok cleared his throat and made answer.
"In the old time long ago, thy father's father,
Opee-Kwan, went away and came back on the
heels of the years. Nor was a place by the fire
denied him. It is said . . ." He paused significantly,
and they hung on his utterance. "It is said," he
repeated, driving his point home with deliberation,
"that Sipsip, his *klooch*, bore him two sons after
he came back."

"But he had no doings with the offshore wind,"

Opee-Kwan retorted. "He went away into the heart of the land, and it is in the nature of things that a man may go on and on into the land."

"And likewise the sea. But that is neither here nor there. It is said . . . that thy father's father told strange tales of the things he saw."

"Ay, strange tales he told."

"I, too, have strange tales to tell," Nam-Bok stated insidiously. And, as they wavered, "And presents likewise."

He pulled from the bidarka a shawl, marvelous of texture and color, and flung it about his mother's shoulders. The women voiced a collective sigh of admiration, and old Bask-Wah-Wan ruffled the gay material and patted it and crooned in childish joy.

"He has tales to tell," Koogah muttered. "And presents," a woman seconded.

And Opee-Kwan knew that his people were eager, and further, he was aware himself of an itching curiosity concerning those untold tales. "The fishing has been good," he said judiciously, "and we have oil in plenty. So come, Nam-Bok, let us feast."

Two of the men hoisted the bidarka on their shoulders and carried it up to the fire. Nam-Bok walked by the side of Opee-Kwan, and the villagers followed after, save those of the women who lingered a moment to lay caressing fingers on the shawl.

There was little talk while the feast went on, though many and curious were the glances stolen at the son of Bask-Wah-Wan. This embarrassed him — not because he was modest of spirit, however, but for the fact that the stench of the seal oil had robbed him of his appetite, and that he keenly desired to conceal his feelings on the subject.

"Eat; thou art hungry," Opee-Kwan commanded, and Nam-Bok shut both his eyes and shoved his fist into the big pot of putrid fish.

"La la, be not ashamed. The seal were many this year, and strong men are ever hungry." And Bask-Wah-Wan sopped a particularly offensive chunk of salmon into the oil and passed it fondly and dripping to her son.

In despair, when premonitory symptoms warned him that his stomach was not so strong as of old, he filled his pipe and struck up a smoke. The people fed on noisily and watched. Few of them could boast of intimate acquaintance with the precious weed, though now and again small quantities and abominable qualities were obtained in trade from the Eskimos to the northward. Koogah, sitting next to him, indicated that he was not averse to taking a draw, and between two mouthfuls, with the oil

77

thick on his lips, sucked away at the amber stem. And thereupon Nam-Bok held his stomach with a shaky hand and declined the proffered return. Koogah could keep the pipe, he said, for he had intended so to honor him from the first. And the people licked their fingers and approved of his liberality.

Opee-Kwan rose to his feet. "And now, O Nam-Bok, the feast is ended, and we would listen concerning the strange things you have seen."

The fisherfolk applauded with their hands, and gathering about them their work, prepared to listen. The men were busy fashioning spears and carving on ivory, while the women scraped the fat from the hides of the hair seal and made them pliable or sewed mukluks with threads of sinew. Nam-Bok's eyes roved over the scene, and there was not the charm about it that his recollection had warranted him to expect. During the years of his wandering he had looked forward to just this scene, and now that it had come he was disappointed. It was a bare and meager life, he deemed, and not to be compared to the one to which he had become used. Still, he would open their eyes a bit, and his own eyes sparkled at the thought.

"Brothers," he began, with the smug complacency of a man about to relate the big things he has done, "it was late summer of many summers back, with much such weather as this promises to be, when I went away. You all remember the day, when the gulls flew low, and the wind blew strong from the land, and I could not hold my bidarka against it. I tied the covering of the bidarka about me so that no water could get in, and all of the night I fought with the storm. And in the morning there was no land — only the sea — and the offshore wind held me close in its arms and bore me along. Three such nights whitened into dawn and showed me no land, and the offshore wind would not let me go.

"And when the fourth day came, I was as a madman. I could not dip my paddle for want of food; and my head went round and round, from the thirst that was upon me. But the sea was no longer angry, and the soft south wind was blowing, and as I looked about me I saw a sight that made me think I was indeed mad."

Nam-Bok paused to pick away a sliver of salmon lodged between his teeth, and the men and women, with idle hands and heads craned forward, waited.

"It was a canoe, a big canoe. If all the canoes I have ever seen were made into one canoe, it would not be so large."

There were exclamations of doubt, and Koogah, whose years were many, shook his head.

"If each bidarka were as a grain of sand," Nam-

Bok defiantly continued, "and if there were as many bidarkas as there be grains of sand in this beach, still would they not make so big a canoe as this I saw on the morning of the fourth day. It was a very big canoe, and it was called a *schooner*. I saw this thing of wonder, this great schooner, coming after me, and on it I saw men . . ."

"Hold, O Nam-Bok!" Opee-Kwan broke in. "What manner of men were they — big men?"

"Nay, mere men like you and me."

"Did the big canoe come fast?"

"Ay."

"The sides were tall, the men short." Opee-Kwan stated the premises with conviction. "And did these men dip with long paddles?"

Nam-Bok grinned. "There were no paddles," he said.

Mouths remained open, and a long silence dropped down. Opee-Kwan borrowed Koogah's pipe for a couple of contemplative sucks. One of the younger women giggled nervously and drew upon herself angry eyes.

"There were no paddles?" Opee-Kwan asked softly, returning the pipe.

"The south wind was behind," Nam-Bok explained.

"But the wind-drift is slow."

"The schooner had wings — thus." He sketched

a diagram of masts and sails in the sand, and the men crowded around and studied it. The wind was blowing briskly, and for more graphic elucidation he seized the corners of his mother's shawl and spread them out till it bellied like a sail. Bask-Wah-Wan scolded and struggled, but was blown down the beach for a score of feet and left breathless and stranded in a heap of driftwood. The men uttered sage grunts of comprehension, but Koogah suddenly tossed back his hoary head.

"Ho! Ho!" he laughed. "A foolish thing, this big canoe! A most foolish thing! The plaything of the wind! Wheresoever the wind goes, it goes too. No man who journeys therein may name the landing beach, for always he goes with the wind, and the wind goes everywhere, but no man knows where."

"It is so," Opee-Kwan supplemented gravely. "With the wind the going is easy, but against the wind a man striveth hard; and for that they had no paddles these men on the big canoe did not strive at all."

"Small need to strive," Nam-Bok cried angrily. "The schooner went likewise against the wind."

"And what said you made the sch — sch — schooner go?" Koogah asked, tripping craftily over the strange word.

"The wind," was the impatient response.

"Then the wind made the sch — sch — schooner

81

go against the wind." Old Koogah dropped an open leer to Opee-Kwan, and, the laughter growing around him, continued: "The wind blows from the south and blows the schooner south. The wind blows against the wind. The wind blows one way and the other at the same time. It is very simple. We understand, Nam-Bok. We clearly understand."

"Thou art a fool!"

"Truth falls from thy lips," Koogah answered meekly. "I was over-long in understanding, and the thing was simple."

But Nam-Bok's face was dark, and he said rapid words which they had never heard before. Bone-scratching and skin-scraping were resumed, but he shut his lips tightly on the tongue that could not be believed.

"This sch — sch — schooner," Koogah imperturbably asked, "it was made of a big tree?"

"It was made of many trees," Nam-Bok snapped shortly. "It was very big."

He lapsed into sullen silence again, and Opee-Kwan nudged Koogah, who shook his head with slow amazement and murmured, "It is very strange."

Nam-Bok took the bait. "That is nothing," he said airily; "you should see the *steamer*. As the grain of sand is to the bidarka, as the bidarka is to the schooner, so the schooner is to the steamer.

Further, the steamer is made of iron. It is all iron."

"Nay, nay, Nam-Bok," cried the head man; "how can that be? Always iron goes to the bottom. For behold, I received an iron knife in trade from the head man of the next village, and yesterday the iron knife slipped from my fingers and went down, down, into the sea. To all things there be law. Never was there one thing outside the law. This we know. And, moreover, we know that things of a kind have the one law, and that all iron has the one law. So unsay thy words, Nam-Bok, that we may yet honor thee."

"It is so," Nam-Bok persisted. "The steamer is all iron and does not sink."

"Nay, nay; this cannot be."

"With my own eyes I saw it."

"It is not in the nature of things."

"But tell me, Nam-Bok," Kookah interrupted, for fear the tale would go no further, "tell me the manner of these men in finding their way across the sea when there is no land by which to steer."

"The sun points out the path."

"But how?"

"At midday the head man of the schooner takes a thing through which his eye looks at the sun, and then he makes the sun climb down out of the sky to the edge of the earth."

"Now this be evil medicine!" cried Opee-Kwan, aghast at the sacrilege. The men held up their hands in horror, and the women moaned. "This be evil medicine. It is not good to misdirect the great sun which drives away the night and gives us the seal, the salmon, and warm weather."

"What if it be evil medicine?" Nam-Bok demanded truculently. "I, too, have looked through the thing at the sun and made the sun climb down out of the sky."

Those who were nearest drew away from him hurriedly, and a woman covered the face of a child at her breast so that his eye might not fall upon it.

"But on the morning of the fourth day, O Nam-Bok," Koogah suggested; "on the morning of the fourth day when the sch — sch — schooner came after thee?"

"I had little strength left in me and could not run away. So I was taken on board and water was poured down my throat and good food given me. Twice, my brothers, you have seen a white man. These men were all white and as many as have I fingers and toes. And when I saw they were full of kindness, I took heart, and I resolved to bring away with me report of all that I saw. And they taught me the work they did, and gave me good food and a place to sleep.

"And day after day we went over the sea, and each day the head man drew the sun down out of the sky and made it tell where we were. And when the waves were kind, we hunted the fur seal and I marveled much, for always did they fling the meat and the fat away and save only the skin."

Opee-Kwan's mouth was twitching violently, and he was about to make denunication of such waste when Koogah kicked him to be still.

"After a weary time, when the sun was gone and the bite of the frost come into the air, the head man pointed the nose of the schooner south. South and east we traveled for days upon days, with never the land in sight, and we were near to the village from which hailed the men . . ."

"How did they know they were near?" Opee-Kwan, unable to contain himself longer, demanded. "There was no land to see."

Nam-Bok glowered on him wrathfully. "Did I not say the head man brought the sun down out of the sky?"

Koogah interposed, and Nam-Bok went on.

"As I say, when we were near to that village a great storm blew up, and in the night we were helpless and knew not where we were . . ."

"Thou hast just said the head man knew . . ."

"Oh, peace, Opee-Kwan. Thou art a fool and cannot understand. As I say, we were helpless in

85

the night, when I heard, above the roar of the storm, the sound of the sea on the beach. And next we struck with a mighty crash and I was in the water, swimming. It was a rock-bound coast, with one patch of beach in many miles, and the law was that I should dig my hands into the sand and draw myself clear of the surf. The other men must have pounded against the rocks, for none of them came ashore but the head man, and him I knew only by the ring on his finger.

"When day came, there being nothing of the schooner, I turned my face to the land and journeyed into it that I might get food and look upon the faces of the people. And when I came to a house I was taken in and given to eat, for I had learned their speech, and the white men are ever kindly. And it was a house bigger than all the houses built by us and our fathers before us."

"It was a mighty house," Koogah said, masking his unbelief with wonder.

"And many houses went into the making of such a house," Opee-Kwan added, taking the cue.

"That is nothing." Nam-Bok shrugged his shoulders in belittling fashion. "As our houses are to that house, so that house was to the houses I was yet to see."

"And they are not big men?"

"Nay; mere men like you and me," Nam-Bok answered. "I had cut a stick that I might walk in comfort, and remembering that I was to bring report to you, my brothers, I cut a notch in the stick for each person who lived in that house. And I stayed there many days, and worked, for which they gave me *money* — a thing of which you know nothing, but which is very good.

"And one day I departed from that place to go farther into the land. And as I walked I met many people, and I cut smaller notches in the stick, that there might be room for all. Then I came upon a strange thing. On the ground before me was a bar of iron, as big in thickness as my arm, and a long step away was another bar of iron——"

"Then wert thou a rich man," Opee-Kwan asserted; "for iron be worth more than anything else in the world. It would have made many knives."

"Nay, it was not mine."

"It was a find, and a find be lawful."

"Not so; the white man had placed it there. And further, these bars were so long that no man could carry them away — so long that as far as I could see there was no end to them."

"Nam-Bok, that is very much iron," Opee-Kwan cautioned.

"Ay, it was hard to believe with my own eyes upon it; but I could not gainsay my eyes. And as I looked I heard . . ." He turned abruptly upon

the head man. "Opee-Kwan, thou hast heard the
sea lion bellow in his anger. Make it plain in thy
mind of as many sea lions as there be waves to the
sea, and make it plain that all these sea lions be
made into one sea lion, and as that one sea lion
would bellow so bellowed the thing I heard."

The fisherfolk cried aloud in astonishment, and
Opee-Kwan's jaw lowered and remained lowered.

"And in the distance I saw a monster like unto
a thousand whales. It was one-eyed, and vomited
smoke, and it snorted with exceeding loudness. I
was afraid and ran with shaking legs along the
path between the bars. But it came with speed of
the wind, this monster, and I leaped the iron bars
with its breath hot on my face . . ."

Opee-Kwan gained control of his jaw again. "And
— and then, O Nam-Bok?"

"Then it came by on the bars, and harmed me
not; and when my legs could hold me up again it
was gone from sight. And it is a very common thing
in that country. Even the women and children are
not afraid. Men make them to do work, these
monsters."

"As we make our dogs do work?" Koogah asked,
with a skeptic twinkle in his eye.

"Ay, as we make our dogs do work."

"And how do they breed these — these things?"
Opee-Kwan questioned.

"They breed not at all. Men fashion them cunningly of iron, and feed them with stone, and give them water to drink. The stone becomes fire, and the water becomes steam, and the steam of the water is the breath of their nostrils, and . . ."

"There, there, O Nam-Bok," Opee-Kwan interrupted. "Tell us of other wonders. We grow tired of this which we may not understand."

"You do not understand?" Nam-Bok asked despairingly.

"Nay, we do not understand," the men and women wailed back. "We cannot understand."

Nam-Bok thought of a combined harvester, and of the machines wherein visions of living men were to be seen, and of the machines from which came the voices of men, and he knew his people could never understand.

"Dare I say I rode this iron monster through the land?" he asked bitterly.

Opee-Kwan threw up his hands, palms outward, in open incredulity. "Say on; say anything. We listen."

"Then did I ride the iron monster, for which I gave money . . ."

"Thou saidst it was fed with stone."

"And likewise, thou fool, I said money was a thing of which you know nothing. As I say, I rode the monster through the land, and through many villages, until I came to a big village on a salt arm of the sea. And the houses shoved their roofs among the stars in the sky, and the clouds drifted by them, and everywhere was much smoke. And the roar of that village was like the roar of the sea in storm, and the people were so many that I flung away my stick and no longer remembered the notches upon it."

"Hadst thou made small notches," Koogah reproved, "thou mightest have brought report."

Nam-Bok whirled upon him in anger. "Had I made small notches! Listen, Koogah, thou scratcher of bone! If I had made small notches neither the stick, nor twenty sticks, could have borne them — nay, not all the driftwood of all the beaches between this village and the next. And if all of you, the women and children as well, were twenty times as many, and if you had twenty hands each, and in each hand a stick and a knife, still the notches could not be cut for the people I saw, so many were they and so fast did they come and go."

"There cannot be so many people in all the world," Opee-Kwan objected, for he was stunned and his mind could not grasp such magnitude of numbers.

"What dost thou know of all the world and how large it is?" Nam-Bok demanded.

"But there cannot be so many people in one place."

"Who art thou to say what can be and what cannot be?"

"It stands to reason there cannot be so many people in one place. Their canoes would clutter the sea till there was no room. And they could empty the sea each day of its fish, and they would not all be fed."

"So it would seem," Nam-Bok made final answer; "yet it was so. With my own eyes I saw, and flung my stick away." He yawned heavily and rose to his feet. "I have paddled far. The day has been long, and I am tired. Now I will sleep, and tomorrow we will have further talk upon the things I have seen."

Bask-Wah-Wan, hobbling fearfully in advance, proud indeed, yet awed by her wonderful son, led him to her igloo and stowed him away among the greasy, ill-smelling furs. But the men lingered by the fire, and a council was held wherein was there much whispering and low-voiced discussion.

An hour passed, and a second, and Nam-Bok slept, and the talk went on. The evening sun dipped toward the northwest, and at eleven at night was nearly due north. Then it was that the head man and the bone-scratcher separated themselves from the council and aroused Nam-Bok. He blinked up into their faces and turned on his side to sleep again. Opee-Kwan gripped him by the arm and kindly but firmly shook his senses back into him.

"Come, Nam-Bok, arise!" he commanded. "It be time."

"Another feast?" Nam-Bok cried. "Nay, I am not hungry. Go on with the eating and let me sleep."

"Time to be gone!" Koogah thundered.

But Opee-Kwan spoke more softly. "Thou wast bidarka-mate with me when we were boys," he said. "Together we first chased the seal and drew the salmon from the traps. And thou didst drag me back to life, Nam-Bok, when the sea closed over me and I was sucked down to the black rocks. Together we hungered and bore the chill of the frost, and together we crawled beneath the one fur and lay close to each other. And because of these things, and the kindness in which I stood to thee, it grieves me sore that thou shouldst return such a remarkable liar. We cannot understand, and our heads be dizzy with the things thou hast spoken. It is not good, and there has been much talk in the council. Wherefore we send thee away, that our heads may remain clear and strong and be not troubled by the unaccountable things."

"These things thou speakest of be shadows," Koogah took up the strain. "From the shadow world thou hast brought them, and to the shadow world thou must return them. Thy bidarka be ready, and the tribespeople wait. They may not sleep until thou art gone."

Nam-Bok was perplexed, but hearkened to the voice of the head man.

"If thou art Nam-Bok," Opee-Kwan was saying, "thou art a fearful and most wonderful liar; if thou art the shadow of Nam-Bok, then thou speakest of shadows, concerning which it is not good that living men have knowledge. This great village thou hast spoken of we deem the village of shadows. Therein flutter the souls of the dead; for the dead be many and the living few. The dead do not come back. Never have the dead come back — save thou with thy wonder-tales. It is not meet that the dead come back, and should we permit it, great trouble may be our portion."

Nam-Bok knew his people well and was aware that the voice of the council was supreme. So he allowed himself to be led down to the water's edge, where he was put aboard his bidarka and a paddle thrust into his hand. A stray wild fowl honked somewhere to seaward, and the surf broke limply and hollowly on the sand. A dim twilight brooded over the land and water, and in the north the sun smoldered, vague and troubled, and draped about with blood-red mists. The gulls were flying low.

The offshore wind blew keen and chill, and the black-massed clouds behind it gave promise of bitter weather.

"Out of the sea thou camest," Opee-Kwan chanted oracularly, "and back into the sea thou goest. Thus is balance achieved and all things brought to law."

Bask-Wah-Wan limped to the froth mark and cried, "I bless thee, Nam-Bok for that thou remembered me."

But Koogah, shoving Nam-Bok clear of the beach, tore the shawl from her shoulders and flung it into the bidarka.

"It is cold in the long nights," she wailed; "and the frost is prone to nip old bones."

"The thing is a shadow," the bone-scratcher answered, "and shadows cannot keep thee warm."

Nam-Bok stood up that his voice might carry. "O Bask-Wah-Wan, mother that bore me!" he called. "Listen to the words of Nam-Bok, thy son. There be room in his bidarka for two, and he would that thou camest with him. For his journey is to where there are fish and oil in plenty. There the frost comes not, and life is easy, and the things of iron do the work of men. Wilt thou come, O Bask-Wah-Wan?"

She debated a moment, while the bidarka drifted swiftly from her, then raised her voice to a quavering treble. "I am old, Nam-Bok, and soon I shall pass down among the shadows. But I have no wish to go before my time. I am old, Nam-Bok, and I am afraid."

A shaft of light shot across the dim-lit sea and wrapped boat and man in a splendor of red and gold. Then a hush fell upon the fisherfolk, and only was heard the moan of the offshore wind and the cries of the gulls flying low in the air.

TO BUILD
A FIRE

5

Day had broken cold and gray, exceedingly cold and gray, when the man turned aside from the main Yukon trail and climbed the high earth bank, where a dim and little-traveled trail led eastward through the fat spruce timberland. It was a steep bank, and he paused for breath at the top, excusing the act to himself by looking at his watch. It was nine o'clock. There was no sun nor hint of sun, though there was not a cloud in the sky. It was a clear day, and yet there seemed an intangible pall over the face of things, a subtle gloom that made the day dark, and that was due to the absence of sun. This fact did not worry the man. He was used to the lack of sun. It had been days since he had seen the sun, and he knew that a few more days must pass before that cheerful orb, due south, would just peep above the skyline and dip immediately from view.

The man flung a look back along the way he had come. The Yukon lay a mile wide and hidden under three feet of ice. On top of this ice were as many feet of snow. It was all pure white, rolling in gentle undulations where the ice jams of the freeze-up had formed. North and south, as far as his eye could see, it was unbroken white, save for a dark hairline that curved and twisted from around the spruce-covered island to the south, and that curved and twisted away into the north, where it disappeared behind another spruce-covered island. This dark hairline was the trail — the main trail — that led south five hundred miles to the Chilcoot Pass, Dyea, and salt water; and that led north seventy miles to Dawson, and still on to the north a thousand miles to Nulato, and finally to St. Michael on Bering Sea, a thousand miles and half a thousand more.

But all this — the mysterious, far-reaching hairline trail, the absence of sun from the sky, the tremendous cold, and the strangeness and weirdness of it all — made no impression on the man. It was not because he was long used to it. He was a newcomer in the land, a *che-cha-quo*, and this was his first winter. The trouble with him was that he was without imagination. He was quick and alert in the things of life, but only in the things, and not in the significances. Fifty degrees below zero meant eighty-odd degrees of frost. Such fact impressed him as being cold and uncomfortable, and that was all. It did not lead him to meditate upon his frailty as a creature of temperature, and upon man's frailty in general, able only to live within certain narrow limits of heat and cold; and from there on it did not lead him to the conjectural field of immortality and man's place in the universe. Fifty degrees below zero stood for a bite of frost that hurt and that must be guarded against by the use of mittens, ear flaps, warm moccasins, and thick socks. Fifty degrees below zero was to him just precisely fifty degrees below zero. That there should be anything more to it than that was a thought that never entered his head.

As he turned to go on, he spat speculatively. There was a sharp, explosive crackle that startled him. He spat again. And again, in the air, before it could fall to the snow, the spittle crackled. He knew that at fifty below spittle crackled in the snow but this spittle had crackled in the air. Undoubtedly it was colder than fifty below — how much colder he did not know. But the temperature did not matter. He was bound for the old claim on the left fork of Henderson Creek, where the boys were already. They had come over across the divide from the Indian Creek country, while he had come the roundabout way to take a look at the possibilities of getting out logs in the spring from the islands in the Yukon. He would be in camp by six o'clock; a bit after dark, it was true, but the boys would be there, a fire would be going, and a hot supper would be ready. As for lunch, he pressed his hand against the protruding bundle under his jacket. It was also under his shirt, wrapped up in a handkerchief and lying against the naked skin. It was the only way to keep the biscuits from freezing. He smiled agreeably to himself as he thought of those biscuits, each cut open and sopped in bacon grease, and each enclosing a generous slice of fried bacon.

He plunged in among the big spruce trees. The trail was faint. A foot of snow had fallen since the last sled has passed over, and he was glad he was without a sled, traveling light. In fact, he carried nothing but the lunch wrapped in the handkerchief. He was surprised, however, at the cold. It certainly was cold, he concluded, as he rubbed his numb nose and cheekbones with his mittened hand. He was a warm-whiskered man, but the hair on his face did not protect the high cheekbones and the eager nose that thrust itself aggressively into the frosty air.

At the man's heels trotted a dog, a big native husky, the proper wolf dog, gray-coated and without any visible or temperamental difference from its brother, the wild wolf. The animal was depressed by the tremendous cold. It knew that it was no time for traveling. Its instinct told it a truer tale than was told to the man by the man's judgment. In reality, it was not merely colder than fifty below zero; it was colder than sixty below, than seventy below. It was seventy-five below zero. Since the freezing point is thirty-two above zero, it meant that one hundred and seven degrees of frost obtained. The dog did not know anything about thermometers. Possibly in its brain there was no sharp consciousness of a condition of very cold such as was in the man's brain. But the brute had its instinct. It experienced a vague but menacing apprehension that subdued it and made it slink along at the man's heels, and that made it question eagerly every unwonted movement of the man as if expecting him to go into camp or to seek shelter somewhere and build a fire. The dog had learned fire, and it wanted fire, or else to burrow under the snow and cuddle its warmth away from the air.

The frozen moisture of its breathing had settled

on its fur in a fine powder of frost, and especially were its jowls, muzzle, and eyelashes whitened by its crystaled breath. The man's red beard and mustache were likewise frosted, but more solidly, the deposit taking the form of ice and increasing with every warm, moist breath he exhaled. Also, the man was chewing tobacco, and the muzzle of ice held his lips so rigidly that he was unable to clear his chin when he expelled the juice. The result was that a crystal beard of the color and solidity of amber was increasing its length on his chin. If he fell down it would shatter itself, like glass, into brittle fragments. But he did not mind the appendage. It was the penalty all tobacco chewers paid in that country, and he had been out before in two cold snaps. They had not been so cold as this, he knew, but by the spirit thermometer at Sixty Mile he knew they had been registered at fifty below and at fifty-five.

He held on through the level stretch of woods for several miles, crossed a wide flat of sedge, and dropped down a bank to the frozen bed of a small stream. This was Henderson Creek, and he knew he was ten miles from the forks. He looked at his watch. It was ten o'clock. He was making four miles an hour, and he calculated that he would arrive at the forks at half-past twelve. He decided to celebrate that event by eating his lunch there.

The dog dropped in again at his heels, with a tail drooping discouragement, as the man swung along the creek bed. The furrow of the old sled trail was plainly visible, but a dozen inches of snow covered the marks of the last runners. In a month no man had come up or down that silent creek. The man held steadily on. He was not much given to thinking, and just then particularly he had nothing to think about save that he would eat lunch at the forks and that at six o'clock he would be in camp with the boys. There was nobody to talk to; and, had there been, speech would have been impossible because of the ice muzzle on his mouth. So he continued monotonously to chew tobacco and to increase the length of his amber beard.

Once in a while the thought reiterated itself that it was very cold and that he had never experienced such cold. As he walked along he rubbed his cheekbones and nose with the back of his mittened hand. He did this automatically, now and again changing hands. But rub as he would, the instant he stopped his cheekbones went numb, and the following instant the end of his nose went numb. He was sure to frost his cheeks; he knew that, and experienced a pang of regret that he had not devised a nose strap of the sort Bud wore in cold snaps. Such a strap passed across the cheeks, as well, and saved them. But it didn't matter much, after all. What

102

were frosted cheeks? A bit painful, that was all; they were never serious.

Empty as the man's mind was of thoughts, he was keenly observant, and he noticed the changes in the creek, the curves and bends and timber jams, and always he sharply noted where he placed his feet. Once, coming around a bend, he shied abruptly, like a startled horse, curved away from the place where he had been walking, and retreated several paces back along the trail. The creek he knew was frozen clear to the bottom — no creek could contain water in that arctic winter — but he knew also that there were springs that bubbled out from the hillsides and ran along under the snow and on top of the ice of the creek. He knew that the coldest snaps never froze these springs, and he knew likewise their danger. They were traps. They hid pools of water under the snow that might be three inches deep, or three feet. Sometimes a skin of ice half an inch thick covered them, and in turn was covered by the snow. Sometimes there were alternate layers of water and ice skin, so that when one broke through he kept on breaking through for a while, sometimes wetting himself to the waist.

That was why he had shied in such panic. He had felt the give under his feet and heard the crackle of a snow-hidden ice skin. And to get his feet wet in such a temperature meant trouble and danger. At the very least it meant delay, for he would be forced to stop and build a fire, and under its protection to bare his feet while he dried his socks and moccasins. He stood and studied the creek bed and its banks, and decided that the flow of water came from the right. He reflected awhile, rubbing his nose and cheeks, then skirted to the left, stepping gingerly and testing the footing for each step. Once clear of the danger, he took a fresh chew of tobacco and swung along at his four-mile gait.

In the course of the next two hours he came upon several similar traps. Usually the snow above the hidden pools had a sunken, candied appearance that advertised the danger. Once again, however, he had a close call; and once, suspecting danger, he compelled the dog to go on in front. The dog did not want to go. It hung back until the man shoved it forward, and then it went quickly across the white, unbroken surface. Suddenly it broke through, floundered to one side, and got away to firmer footing. It had wet its forefeet and legs, and almost immediately the water that clung to it turned to ice. It made quick efforts to lick the ice off its legs, then dropped down in the snow and began to bite out the ice that had formed between the toes. This was a matter of instinct. To permit the ice to remain would mean sore feet. It did not know this. It merely obeyed the mysterious prompting that arose from the deep crypts of its being. But the man knew, having achieved a judgment on the subject, and he removed the mitten from his right hand and helped tear out the ice particles. He did not expose his fingers more than a minute, and was astonished at the swift numbness that smote them. It certainly was cold. He pulled on the mitten hastily, and beat the hand savagely across his chest.

At twelve o'clock, the day was at its brightest. Yet the sun was too far south on its winter journey to clear the horizon. The bulge of the earth intervened between it and Henderson Creek, where the man walked under a clear sky at noon and cast no shadow. At half-past twelve, to the minute, he arrived at the forks of the creek. He was pleased at the speed he had made. If he kept it up, he would certainly be with the boys by six. He unbuttoned his jacket and shirt and drew forth his lunch. The action consumed no more than a quarter of a minute, yet in that brief moment the numbness laid hold of the exposed fingers. He did not put the mitten on, but, instead, struck the fingers a dozen sharp smashes against his leg. Then he sat down on a snow-covered log to eat. The sting that followed upon the striking of his fingers against his leg ceased so quickly that he was startled. He had had no chance to take a bite of biscuit. He struck

105

the fingers repeatedly and returned them to the mitten, baring the other hand for the purpose of eating. He tried to take a mouthful, but the ice-muzzle prevented. He had forgotten to build a fire and thaw out. He chuckled at his foolishness, and as he chuckled he noted the numbness creeping into the exposed fingers. Also, he noted that the stinging which had first come to his toes when he sat down was already passing away. He wondered whether the toes were warm or numb. He moved them inside the moccasins and decided that they were numb.

He pulled the mitten on hurriedly and stood up. He was a bit frightened. He stamped up and down until the stinging returned into the feet. It certainly was cold, was his thought. That man from Sulphur Creek had spoken the truth when telling how cold it sometimes got in the country. And he had laughed at him at the time! That showed one must not be too sure of things. There was no mistake about it, it *was* cold. He strode up and down, stamping his feet and threshing his arms, until reassured by the returning warmth. Then he got out matches and proceeded to make a fire. From the undergrowth, where high water of the previous spring had lodged a supply of seasoned twigs, he got his firewood. Working carefully from a small beginning, he soon had a roaring fire, over which he thawed the ice from his face and in the protection of which he ate his biscuits. For the moment the cold of space was outwitted. The dog took satisfaction in the fire, stretching out close enough for warmth and far enough away to escape being singed.

When the man had finished, he filled his pipe and took his comfortable time over a smoke. Then he pulled on his mittens, settled the ear flaps of his cap firmly about his ears, and took the creek trail up the left fork. The dog was disappointed and yearned back toward the fire. This man did not know cold. Possibly all the generations of his ancestry had been ignorant of cold, of real cold, of cold one hundred and seven degrees below freezing point. But the dog knew; all its ancestry knew, and it had inherited the knowledge. And it knew that it was not good to walk abroad in such fearful cold. It was the time to lie snug in a hole in the snow and wait for a curtain of cloud to be drawn across the face of outer space whence this cold came. On the other hand, there was no keen intimacy between the dog and the man. The one was the toil-slave of the other, and the only caresses it had ever received were the caresses of the whiplash and of harsh and menacing throat sounds that threatened the whiplash. So the dog made no effort to communicate its apprehension to the man. It was not concerned in the welfare of the man; it was for its own sake that it yearned back toward the fire. But the man whistled, and spoke to it with the sound of whiplashes, and the dog swung in at the man's heels and followed after.

The man took a chew of tobacco and proceeded to start a new amber beard. Also, his moist breath quickly powdered with white his mustache, eyebrows, and lashes. There did not seem to be so many springs on the left fork of the Henderson, and for half an hour the man saw no signs of any. And then it happened. At a place where there were no signs, where the soft, unbroken snow seemed to advertise solidity beneath, the man broke through. It was not deep. He wet himself halfway to the knees before he floundered out to the firm crust.

He was angry, and cursed his luck aloud. He had hoped to get into camp with the boys at six o'clock, and this would delay him an hour, for he would have to build a fire and dry out his footgear. This was imperative at that low temperature — he knew that much; and he turned aside to the bank, which he climbed. On top, tangled in the underbrush about the trunks of several small spruce trees, was a high-water deposit of dry firewood — sticks and twigs, principally, but also larger portions of seasoned branches and fine, dry, last-year's grasses. He threw down several large pieces on top of the snow. This served for a foundation and prevented the young flame from drowning itself in the snow it otherwise would melt. The flame he got by touching a match to a small shred of birch bark that he took from his pocket. This burned even more readily than paper. Placing it on the foundation, he fed the young flame with wisps of dry grass and with the tiniest dry twigs.

He worked slowly and carefully, keenly aware of his danger. Gradually, as the flame grew stronger, he increased the size of the twigs with which he fed it. He squatted in the snow, pulling the twigs out from their entanglement in the brush and feeding directly to the flame. He knew there must be no failure. When it is seventy-five below zero, a man must not fail in his first attempt to build a fire — that is, if his feet are wet. If his feet are dry, and he fails, he can run along the trail for half a mile and restore his circulation. But the circulation of wet and freezing feet cannot be restored by running when it is seventy-five below. No matter how fast he runs, the wet feet will freeze the harder.

All this the man knew. The old-timer on Sulphur Creek had told him about it the previous fall, and now he was appreciating the advice. Already all sensation had gone out of his feet. To build the fire he had been forced to remove his mittens, and the fingers had quickly gone numb. His pace of four miles an hour had kept his heart pumping blood to the surface of his body and to all the extremities. But the instant he stopped, the action of the pump eased down. The cold of space smote the unprotected tip of the planet, and he, being on that unprotected tip, received the full force of the blow. The blood of his body recoiled before it. The blood was alive, like the dog, and like the dog it wanted to hide away and cover itself up from the fearful cold. So long as he walked four miles an hour, he pumped that blood, willy-nilly, to the surface; but now it ebbed away and sank down into the recesses of his body. The extremities were the first to feel its absence. His wet feet froze the faster, and his exposed fingers numbed the faster, though they had not yet begun to freeze. Nose and cheeks were already freezing, while the skin of all his body chilled as it lost its blood.

But he was safe. Toes and nose and cheeks would be only touched by the frost, for the fire was beginning to burn with strength. He was feeding it with twigs the size of his finger. In another minute he would be able to feed it with branches the size of his wrist, and then he could remove his wet footgear, and while it dried he could keep his naked feet warm by the fire, rubbing them at first, of course, with snow. The fire was a success. He was safe. He remembered the advice of the old-timer on Sulphur Creek, and smiled. The old-timer had been very serious in laying down the law that no man must travel alone in the Klondike after fifty below. Well, here he was; he had had the accident; he was alone; and he had saved himself. Those old-timers were rather womanish, some of them, he thought. All a man had to do was to keep his head, and he was all right. Any man who was a man could travel alone. But it was surprising, the rapidity with which his cheeks and nose were freezing. And he had not thought his fingers could go lifeless in so short a time. Lifeless they were, for he could scarcely make them move together to grip a twig, and they seemed remote from his body and from him. When he touched a twig, he had to look and see whether or not he had hold of it. The wires were pretty well down between him and his finger ends.

All of which counted for little. There was the fire, snapping and crackling and promising life with every dancing flame. He started to untie his moccasins. They were coated with ice. The thick German socks were like sheaths of iron halfway to the knees; and the moccasin strings were like rods of steel all twisted and knotted as by some conflagration. For a moment he tugged with his numb fingers, then, realizing the folly of it, he drew his sheath knife.

But before he could cut the strings, it happened.

111

It was his own fault or, rather, his mistake. He should not have built the fire under the spruce tree. He should have built it in the open. But it had been easier to pull the twigs from the brush and drop them directly on the fire. Now the tree under which he had done this carried a weight of snow on its boughs. No wind had blown for weeks, and each bough was fully weighted. Each time he had pulled a twig he had communicated a slight agitation to the tree — an imperceptible agitation, so far as he was concerned, but an agitation sufficient to bring about the disaster. High up in the tree one bough capsized its load of snow. This fell on the boughs beneath, capsizing them. This process continued, spreading out and involving the whole tree. It grew like an avalanche, and it descended without warning upon the man and the fire, and the fire was blotted out! Where it had burned was a mantle of fresh and disordered snow.

The man was shocked. It was as though he had just heard his own sentence of death. For a moment he sat and stared at the spot where the fire had been. Then he grew very calm. Perhaps the old-timer on Sulphur Creek was right. If he had only had a trail mate he would have been in no danger now. The trail mate could have built the fire. Well, it was up to him to build the fire over again, and this second time there must be no failure. Even if he succeeded, he would most likely lose some toes. His feet must be badly frozen by now, and there would be some time before the second fire was ready.

Such were his thoughts, but he did not sit and think about them. He was busy all the time they were passing through his mind. He made a new foundation for a fire, this time in the open, where no treacherous tree could blot it out. Next, he gathered dry grasses and tiny twigs from the high-water flotsam. He could not bring his fingers together to pull them out, but he was able to gather them by the handful. In this way he got many rotten twigs and bits of green moss that were undesirable, but it was the best he could do. He worked methodically, even collecting an armful of the larger branches to be used later when the fire gathered strength. And all the while the dog sat and watched him, a certain yearning wistfulness in its eyes, for it looked upon him as the fire-provider, and the fire was slow in coming.

When all was ready, the man reached in his pocket for a second piece of birch bark. He knew the bark was there, and, though he could not feel it with his fingers, he could hear its crisp rustling as he fumbled for it. Try as he would, he could not clutch hold of it. And all the time, in his consciousness, was the knowledge that each instant his feet

113

were freezing. This thought tended to put him in a panic, but he fought against it and kept calm. He pulled on his mittens with his teeth, and threshed his arms back and forth, beating his hands with all his might against his sides. He did this sitting down, and he stood up to do it; and all the while the dog sat in the snow, its wolf-brush of a tail curled around warmly over its forefeet, its sharp wolf ears pricked forward intently as it watched the man. And the man, as he beat and thrashed with his arms and hands, felt a great surge of envy as he regarded the creature that was warm and secure in its natural covering.

After a time he was aware of the first faraway signals of sensation in his beaten fingers. The faint tingling grew stronger till it evolved into a stinging ache that was excruciating, but which the man hailed with satisfaction. He stripped the mitten from his right hand and fetched forth the birch bark. The exposed fingers were quickly going numb again. Next he brought out his bunch of sulphur matches. But the tremendous cold had already driven the life out of his fingers. In his effort to separate one match from the others, the whole bunch fell in the snow. He tried to pick it out of the snow, but failed. The dead fingers could neither touch nor clutch. He was very careful. He drove the thought of his freezing feet, nose, and cheeks, out of his mind, devoting his whole soul to the matches. He watched, using the sense of vision in place of that of touch, and when he saw his fingers on each side the bunch, he closed them — that is, he willed to close them, for the wires were down, and the fingers did not obey. He pulled the mitten on the right hand, and beat it fiercely against his knee. Then, with both mittened hands, he scooped the bunch of matches, along with much snow, into his lap. Yet he was no better off.

After some manipulation he managed to get the bunch between the heels of his mittened hands. In this fashion he carried it to his mouth. The ice crackled and snapped when by a violent effort he opened his mouth. He drew the lower jaw in, curled the upper lip out of the way, and scraped the bunch with his upper teeth in order to separate a match. He succeeded in getting one, which he dropped on his lap. He was no better off. He could not pick it up. Then he devised a way. He picked it up in his teeth and scratched it on his leg. Twenty times he scratched before he succeeded in lighting it. As it flamed he held with his teeth to the birch bark. But the burning brimstone went up his nostrils and into his lungs, causing him to cough spasmodically. The match fell into the snow and went out.

The old-timer on Sulphur Creek was right, he

thought in the moment of controlled despair that ensued: after fifty below, a man should travel with a partner. He beat his hands, but failed in exciting any sensation. Suddenly he bared both hands, removing the mittens with his teeth. He caught the whole bunch between the heels of his hands. His arm-muscles not being frozen enabled him to press the hand heels tightly against the matches. Then he scratched the bunch along his leg. It flared into flame, seventy sulphur matches at once! There was no wind to blow them out. He kept his head to one side to escape the strangling fumes, and held the blazing bunch to the birch bark. As he so held it, he became aware of sensation in his hand. His flesh was burning. He could smell it. Deep down below the surface he could feel it. The sensation developed into pain that grew acute. And still he endured it, holding the flame of the matches clumsily to the bark that would not light readily because his own burning hands were in the way, absorbing most of the flame.

At last, when he could endure no more, he jerked his hands apart. The blazing matches fell sizzling into the snow, but the birch bark was alight. He began laying dry grasses and the tinest twigs on the flame. He could not pick and choose, for he had to lift the fuel between the heels of his hands. Small pieces of rotten wood and green moss clung to the twigs, and he bit them off as well as he could with his teeth. He cherished the flame carefully and awkwardly. It meant life, and it must not perish. The withdrawal of blood from the surface of his body now made him begin to shiver, and he grew more awkward. A large piece of green moss fell squarely on the little fire. He tried to poke it out with his fingers, but his shivering frame made him poke too far, and he disrupted the nucleus of the little fire, the burning grasses and tiny twigs separating and scattering. He tried to poke them together again, but in spite of the tenseness of the effort, his shivering got away with him, and the twigs were hopelessly scattered. Each twig gushed a puff of smoke and went out. The fire-provider had failed. As he looked apathetically about him, his eyes chanced on the dog, sitting across the ruins of the fire from him, in the snow, making restless, hunching movements, slightly lifting one forefoot and then the other, shifting its weight back and forth on them with wistful eagerness.

The sight of the dog put a wild idea into his head. He remembered the tale of the man, caught in a blizzard, who killed a steer and crawled inside the carcass, and so was saved. He would kill the dog and bury his hands in the warm body until the numbness went out of them. Then he could build another fire. He spoke to the dog, calling it to him; but in his voice was a strange note of fear that frightened the animal, who had never known the man to speak in such a way before. Something was the matter, and its suspicious nature sensed danger — it knew not what the danger, but somewhere, somehow, in its brain arose an apprehension of the man. It flattened its ears down at the sound of the man's voice, and its restless, hunching movements and the liftings and shiftings of its forefeet became more pronounced; but it would not come to the man. He got on his hands and knees and crawled toward the dog. This unusual posture again excited suspicion, and the animal sidled mincingly away.

The man sat up in the snow for a moment and struggled for calmness. Then he pulled on his mittens, by means of his teeth, and got up on his feet. He glanced down at first in order to assure himself that he was really standing up, for the absence of sensation in his feet left him unrelated to the earth. His erect position in itself started to drive the webs of suspicion from the dog's mind; and when he spoke peremptorily, with the sound of whiplashes in his voice, the dog rendered its customary allegiance and came to him. As it came within reaching distance, the man lost his control. His arms flashed out to the dog, and he experienced genuine surprise when he discovered that his hands could not clutch, that there was neither bend nor feeling in the fingers. He had forgotten for the moment that they were frozen and that they were freezing more and more. All this happened quickly, and before the animal could get away, he encircled its body with his arms. He sat down in the snow, and in this fashion held the dog, while it snarled and whined and struggled.

But it was all he could do, hold its body encircled in his arms and sit there. He realized that he could not kill the dog. There was no way to do it. With his helpless hands he could neither draw nor hold his sheath knife nor throttle the animal. He released it, and it plunged wildly away, with tail between its legs, and still snarling. It halted forty feet away and surveyed him curiously, with ears sharply pricked forward. The man looked down at his hands in order to locate them, and found them hanging on the ends of his arms. It struck him as curious that one should have to use his eyes in order to find out where his hands were. He began thrashing his arms back and forth, beating the mittened hands against his sides. He did this for five minutes, violently, and his heart pumped enough blood up to the surface to put a stop to his shivering. But no sensation was aroused in the hands. He had an impression that they hung like weights on the ends of his arms, but when he

119

tried to run the impression down, he could not find it.

A certain fear of death, dull and oppressive, came to him. This fear quickly became poignant as he realized that it was no longer a mere matter of freezing his fingers and toes, or of losing his hands and feet, but that it was a matter of life and death with the chances against him. This threw him into a panic, and he turned and ran up the creek bed along the old, dim trail. The dog joined in behind and kept up with him. He ran blindly, without intention, in fear such as he had never known in his life. Slowly, as he ploughed and floundered through the snow, he began to see things again — the banks of the creek, the old timber jams, the leafless aspens, and the sky. The running made him feel better. He did not shiver. Maybe, if he ran on, his feet would thaw out; and, anyway, if he ran far enough, he would reach camp and the boys. Without doubt he would lose some fingers and toes and some of his face; but the boys would take care of him, and save the rest of him when he got there. And at the same time there was another thought in his mind that said he would never get to the camp and the boys; that it was too many miles away, that the freezing had too great a start on him, and that he would soon be stiff and dead. This thought he kept in the background and refused to consider. Sometimes it pushed itself forward and demanded to be heard, but he thrust it back and strove to think of other things.

It struck him as curious that he could run at all on feet so frozen that he could not feel them when they struck the earth and took the weight of his body. He seemed to himself to skim along above the surface, and to have no connection with the earth. Somewhere he had once seen a winged Mercury, and he wondered if Mercury felt as he felt when skimming over the earth.

His theory of running until he reached camp and the boys had one flaw in it: he lacked the endurance. Several times he stumbled, and finally he tottered, crumpled up, and fell. When he tried to rise, he failed. He must sit and rest, he decided, and next time he would merely walk and keep on going. As he sat and regained his breath, he noted that he was feeling quite warm and comfortable. He was not shivering, and it even seemed that a warm glow had come to his chest and trunk. And yet, when he touched his nose or cheeks, there was no sensation. Running would not thaw them out. Nor would it thaw out his hands and feet. Then the thought came to him that the frozen portions of his body must be extending. He tried to keep this thought down, to forget it, to think of something else; he was aware of the panicky feeling that it caused, and he was afraid of the panic. But the thought asserted itself, and persisted, until it produced a vision of his body totally frozen. This was too much, and he made another wild run along the trail. Once he slowed down to a walk, but the thought of the freezing extending itself made him run again.

And all the time the dog ran with him, at his heels. When he fell down a second time, it curled its tail over its forefeet and sat in front of him, facing him, curiously eager and intent. The warmth and security of the animal angered him, and he cursed it till it flattened down its ears appeasingly. This time the shivering came more quickly upon the man. He was losing in his battle with the frost. It was creeping into his body from all sides. The thought of it drove him on, but he ran no more than a hundred feet, when he staggered and pitched headlong. It was his last panic. When he had recovered his breath and control, he sat up and entertained in his mind the conception of meeting death with dignity. However, the conception did not come to him in such terms. His idea of it was that he had been making a fool of himself, running around like a chicken with its head cut off — such was the simile that occurred to him. Well, he was bound to freeze anyway, and he might as well take it decently. With this new-found peace of mind came the first glimmerings of drowsiness. A good idea, he thought, to sleep off to death. It was like taking an anesthetic. Freezing was not so bad as people thought. There were lots worse ways to die.

He pictured the boys finding his body next day. Suddenly he found himself with them, coming along the trail and looking for himself. And, still with them, he came around a turn in the trail and found himself lying in the snow. He did not belong with himself any more, for even then he was out of himself, standing with the boys and looking at himself in the snow. It certainly was cold, was his thought. When he got back to the States he could tell the folks what real cold was. He drifted on from this to a vision of the old-timer on Sulphur Creek. He could see him quite clearly, warm and comfortable, and smoking a pipe.

"You were right, old hoss; you were right," the man mumbled to the old-timer of Sulphur Creek.

Then the man drowsed off into what seemed to him the most comfortable and satisfying sleep he had ever known. The dog sat facing him and waiting. The brief day drew to a close in a long, slow twilight. There were no signs of a fire to be made, and, besides, never in the dog's experience had it known a man to sit like that in the snow and make no fire. As the twilight drew on, its eager yearning for the fire mastered it, and with a great lifting and shifting of forefeet, it whined softly, then flattened its ears down in anticipation of being chidden by the man. But the man remained silent. Later, the dog whined loudly. And still later it crept close to the man and caught the scent of death. This made the animal bristle and back away. A little longer it delayed, howling under the stars that leaped and danced and shone brightly in the cold sky. Then it turned and trotted up the trail in the direction of the camp it knew, where were the other food-providers and fire-providers.

THE
UNEXPECTED

6

I⊤ ɪꜱ a simple matter to see the obvious, to do the expected. The tendency of the individual life is to be static rather than dynamic, and this tendency is made into a propulsion by civilization, where the obvious only is seen, and the unexpected rarely happens. When the unexpected does happen, however, and when it is of sufficiently grave import, the unfit perish. They do not see what is not obvious, are unable to do the unexpected, are incapable of adjusting their well-groomed lives to other and strange grooves. In short, when they come to the end of their own groove, they die.

On the other hand, there are those who make

toward survival, the fit individuals who escape from the rule of the obvious and the expected and adjust their lives to no matter what strange grooves they may stray into, or into which they may be forced. Such an individual was Edith Whittlesey. She was born in a rural district of England, where life proceeds by rule of thumb and the unexpected is so very unexpected that when it happens it is looked upon as an immorality. She went into service early, and while yet a young woman, by rule-of-thumb progression, she became a lady's maid.

The effect of civilization is to impose human law upon environment until it becomes machinelike in its regularity. The objectionable is eliminated, the inevitable is foreseen. One is not even made wet by the rain nor cold by the frost; while death instead of stalking about gruesome and accidental, becomes a prearranged pageant, moving along a well-oiled groove to the family vault, where the hinges are kept from rusting, and the dust from the air is swept continually away.

Such was the environment of Edith Whittlesey. Nothing happened. It could scarcely be called a happening, when, at the age of twenty-five, she accompanied her mistress on a bit of travel to the United States. The groove merely changed its direction. It was still the same groove and well oiled.

It was a groove that bridged the Atlantic with uneventfulness, so that the ship was not a ship in the midst of the sea, but a capacious, many-corridored hotel that moved swiftly and placidly, crushing the waves into submission with its colossal bulk until the sea was a millpond, monotonous with quietude. And at the other side the groove continued on over the land—a well-disposed, respectable groove that supplied hotels at every stopping place, and hotels on wheels between the stopping places.

In Chicago, while her mistress saw one side of social life, Edith Whittlesey saw another side; and when she left her lady's service and became Edith Nelson, she betrayed, perhaps faintly, her ability to grapple with the unexpected and to master it. Hans Nelson, immigrant, Swede by birth and carpenter by occupation, had in him that Teutonic unrest that drives the race ever westward on its great adventure. He was a large-muscled, stolid sort of a man, in whom little imagination was coupled with immense initiative, and who possessed, withal, loyalty and affection as sturdy as his own strength.

"When I have worked hard and saved me some money, I will go to Colorado," he had told Edith on the day after their wedding. A year later they were in Colorado, where Hans Nelson saw his first mining and caught the mining fever himself. His prospecting led him through the Dakotas, Idaho, and eastern Oregon, and on into the mountains of British Columbia. In camp and on trail, Edith Nelson was always with him, sharing his luck, his hardship, and his toil. The short step of the house-reared woman she exchanged for the long stride of the mountaineer. She learned to look upon danger clear-eyed and with understanding, losing forever that panic fear which is bred of ignorance and which afflicts the city-reared, making them as silly as silly horses, so that they await fate in frozen horror instead of grappling with it, or stampede in blind self-destroying terror which clutters the way with their crushed carcasses.

Edith Nelson met the unexpected at every turn of the trail, and she trained her vision so that she saw in the landscape, not the obvious, but the concealed. She, who had never cooked in her life, learned to make bread without the mediation of hops, yeast, or baking powder, and to bake bread, top and bottom, in a frying-pan before an open fire. And when the last cup of flour was gone and the last rind of bacon, she was able to rise to the occasion, and of moccasins and the softer-tanned bits of leather in the outfit to make a grubstake substitute that somehow held a man's soul in his body and enabled him to stagger on. She learned to pack a horse as well as a man—a task to break the heart and the pride of any city dweller, and she knew how to throw the hitch best suited for any particular kind of pack. Also, she could build a fire of wet wood in a downpour of rain and not lose her temper. In short, in all its guises she mastered the unexpected. But the Great Unexpected was yet to come into her life and put its test upon her.

The gold-seeking tide was flooding northward into Alaska, and it was inevitable that Hans Nelson and his wife should be caught up by the stream and swept toward the Klondike. The fall of 1897 found them at Dyea, but without the money to carry an outfit across Chilcoot Pass and float it down to Dawson. So Hans Nelson worked at his trade that winter and helped rear the mushroom outfitting town of Skagway.

He was on the edge of things, and throughout the winter he heard all Alaska calling to him. Latuya Bay called loudest, so that the summer of 1898 found him and his wife threading the mazes of the broken coast line in seventy-foot Siwash canoes. With them were Indians, also three other men. The Indians landed them and their supplies in a lonely bight of land a hundred miles or so beyond Latuya Bay, and returned to Skagway; but the three other men remained, for they were members of the organized party. Each had put an equal share of capital into the outfitting, and the profits were to be divided equally. In that Edith Nelson undertook to cook for the outfit, a man's share was to be her portion.

First, spruce trees were cut down and a three-room cabin constructed. To keep this cabin was Edith Nelson's task. The task of the men was to search for gold, which they did; and to find gold, which they likewise did. It was not a startling find, merely a low-pay placer where long hours of severe toil earned each man between fifteen and twenty dollars a day. The brief Alaskan summer protracted itself beyond its usual length, and they took advantage of the opportunity, delaying their return to Skagway to the last moment. And then it was too late. Arrangements had been made to accompany the several dozen local Indians on their fall trading trip down the coast. The Siwashes had waited for the white people until the eleventh hour, and then departed. There was no course left the party but to wait for chance transportation. In the meantime, the claim was cleaned up and fire-wood stocked in.

The Indian summer had dreamed on and on, and then, suddenly, with the sharpness of bugles, winter came. It came in a single night, and the miners awoke to howling wind, driving snow, and freezing water. Storm followed storm, and between the storms there was the silence, broken only by the boom of the surf on the desolate shore, where the salt spray rimmed the beach with frozen white.

All went well in the cabin. Their gold dust had weighed up something like eight thousand dollars, and they could not but be contented. The men made snowshoes, hunted fresh meat for the larder, and in the long evenings played endless games of whist and pedro. Now that the mining had ceased, Edith Nelson turned over the fire-building and the dish-washing to the men, while she darned their socks and mended their clothes.

There was no grumbling, no bickering, nor petty quarreling in the little cabin, and they often congratulated one another on the general happiness of the party. Hans Nelson was stolid and easygoing, while Edith had long before won his unbounded admiration by her capacity for getting on with people. Harkey, a long, lank Texan, was unusually friendly for one with a saturnine disposition, and, as long as his theory that gold grew was not challenged, was quite companionable. The fourth member of the party, Michael Dennin, contributed his Irish wit to the gayety of the cabin. He was a large, powerful man, prone to sudden rushes of anger over little things, and of unfailing good humor under the stress and strain of big things. The fifth and last member, Dutchy, was the willing butt of the party. He even went out of his way to raise a laugh at his own expense in order to keep things cheerful. His deliberate aim in life seemed to be that of a maker of laughter. No serious quarrel had ever vexed the serenity of the party; and, now that each had sixteen hundred dollars to show for a short summer's work, there reigned the well-fed, contented spirit of prosperity.

And then the unexpected happened. They had just sat down to the breakfast table. Though it was already eight o'clock (late breakfasts had followed naturally upon cessation of the steady work at mining) a candle in the neck of a bottle lighted the meal. Edith and Hans sat at each end of the table. On one side, with their backs to the door, sat Harkey and Dutchy. The place on the other side was vacant. Dennin had not yet come in.

Hans Nelson looked at the empty chair, shook his head slowly, and, with a ponderous attempt at humor, said: "Always is he first at the grub. It is very strange. Maybe he is sick."

"Where is Michael?" Edith asked.

"Got up a little ahead of us and went outside," Harkey answered.

Dutchy's face beamed mischeviously. He pretended knowledge of Dennin's absence, and affected a mysterious air, while they clamored for information. Edith, after a peep into the men's bunkroom, returned to the table. Hans looked at her, and she shook her head.

"He was never late at mealtime before," she remarked.

"I cannot understand," said Hans. "Always has he the great appetite like the horse."

"It is too bad," Dutchy said, with a sad shake of his head.

They were beginning to make merry over their comrade's absence.

"It is a great pity!" Dutchy volunteered.

"What?" they demanded in chorus.

"Poor Michael," was the mournful reply.

"Well, what's wrong with Michael?" Harkey asked.

"He is not hungry no more," wailed Dutchy. "He has lost der appetite. He do not like der grub."

"Not from the way he pitches into it up to his ears," remarked Harkey.

"He does dot shust to be politeful to Mrs. Nelson," was Dutchy's quick retort. "I know, I know, and it is too pad. Why is he not here? Pecause he haf gone out. Why haf he gone out? For der defelopment of der appetite. How does he defelop der appetite? He walks barefoots in der snow. Ach! don't I know? It is der way der rich peoples chases after der appetite when it is no more and is running away. Michael haf sixteen hundred dollars. He is

133

rich peoples. He haf no appetite. Derefore, pecause, he is chasing der appetite. Shust you open der door und you will see his barefoots in der snow. No, you will not see der appetite. Dot is shust his trouble. When he sees der appetite he will catch it und come to preakfast."

They burst into loud laughter at Dutchy's nonsense. The sound had scarcely died away when the door opened and Dennin came in. All turned to look at him. He was carrying a shotgun. Even as they looked, he lifted it to his shoulder and fired twice. At the first shot Dutchy sank upon the table, overturning his mug of coffee, his yellow mop of hair dabbling in his plate of mush. His forehead, which pressed upon the near edge of the plate, tilted the plate up against his hair at an angle of forty-five degrees. Harkey was in the air, in his spring to his feet, at the second shot, and he pitched face down upon the floor, his "My God!" gurgling and dying in his throat.

It was the unexpected. Hans and Edith were stunned. They sat at the table with bodies tense, their eyes fixed in a fascinated gaze upon the murderer. Dimly they saw him through the smoke of the powder, and in the silence nothing was to be heard save the drip-drip of Dutchy's spilled coffee on the floor. Dennin threw open the breech of the shotgun, ejecting the empty shells. Holding the gun with one hand, he reached with the other into his pocket for fresh shells.

He was thrusting the shells into the gun when Edith Nelson was aroused to action. It was patent that he intended to kill Hans and her. For a space of possibly three seconds of time she had been dazed and paralyzed by the horrible and inconceivable form in which the unexpected had made its appearance. Then she rose to it and grappled with it. She grappled with it concretely, making a cat-like leap for the murderer and gripping his neck-cloth with both her hands. The impact of her body sent him stumbling backward several steps. He tried to shake her loose and still retain his hold on the gun. This was awkward, for her firm-fleshed body had become a cat's. She threw herself to one side, and with her grip at his throat nearly jerked him to the floor. He straightened himself and whirled swiftly. Still faithful to her hold, her body followed the circle of his whirl so that her feet left the floor, and she swung through the air fastened to his throat by her hands. The whirl culminated in a collision with a chair, and the man and woman crashed to the floor in a wild struggling fall that extended itself across half the length of the room.

Hans Nelson was half a second behind his wife in rising to the unexpected. His nerve processes and mental processes were slower than hers. His was the grosser organism, and it had taken him half a second longer to perceive, and determine, and proceed to do. She had already flown at Dennin and gripped his throat, when Hans sprang to his feet. But her coolness was not his. He was in a blind fury, a berserk rage. At the instant he sprang from his chair his mouth opened and there issued forth a sound that was half roar, half bellow. The whirl of the two bodies had already started, and still roaring, or bellowing, he pursued this whirl down the room, overtaking it when it fell to the floor.

Hans hurled himself upon the prostrate man, striking madly with his fists. They were sledge-like blows, and when Edith felt Dennin's body relax she loosed her grip and rolled clear. She lay on the floor, panting and watching. The fury of blows continued to rain down. Dennin did not seem to mind the blows. He did not even move. Then it dawned upon her that he was unconscious. She cried out to Hans to stop. She cried out again. But he paid no heed to her voice. She caught him by the arm, but her clinging to it merely impeded his effort.

It was no reasoned impulse that stirred her to do what she then did. Nor was it a sense of pity, not obedience to the "Thou shalt not" of religion. Rather was it some sense of law, an ethic of her

race and early environment, that compelled her to
interpose her body between her husband and the
helpless murderer. It was not until Hans knew he
was striking his wife that he ceased. He allowed
himself to be shoved away by her much the same
way that a ferocious but obedient dog allows itself
to be shoved away by its master. The analogy went
even farther. Deep in his throat, in an animal-
like way, Hans's rage still rumbled, and several
times he made as though to spring back upon his
prey and was only prevented by the woman's swiftly interposed body.

Back and farther back Edith shoved her husband.
She had never seen him in such a condition, and she
was more frightened of him than she had been of
Dennin in the thick of the struggle. She could not
believe that this raging beast was her Hans, and
with a shock she became suddenly aware of a
shrinking, instinctive fear that he might snap her
hand in his teeth like any wild animal. For some
seconds, unwilling to hurt her, yet dogged in his
desire to return to the attack, Hans dodged back
and forth. But she resolutely dodged with him, until
the first glimmerings of reason returned and he
gave over.

Both crawled to their feet. Hans staggered back
against the wall, where he leaned, his face working, in his throat the deep and continuous rumble

137

that died away with the seconds and at last ceased. The time for the reaction had come. Edith stood in the middle of the floor, wringing her hands, panting and gasping, her whole body trembling violently.

Hans looked at nothing, but Edith's eyes wandered wildly from detail to detail of what had taken place. Dennin lay without movement. The overturned chair, hurled onward in the mad whirl, lay near him. Partly under him lay the shotgun, still broken open at the breech. Spilling out of his right hand were the two cartridges which he had failed to put into the gun and which he had clutched until consciousness left him. Harkey lay on the floor, face downward, where he had fallen; while Dutchy rested forward on the table, his yellow mop of hair buried in his mush plate, the plate itself still tilted at an angle of forty-five degrees. This tilted plate fascinated her. Why did it not fall down? It was ridiculous. It was not in the nature of things for a mush plate to upend itself on the table, even if a man or so had been killed.

She glanced back at Dennin, but her eyes returned to the tilted plate. It was so ridiculous! She felt a hysterical impulse to laugh. Then she noticed the silence, and forgot the plate in a desire for something to happen. The monotonous drip of the coffee from the table to the floor merely emphasized the silence. Why did not Hans do something? say something? She looked at him and was about to speak, when she discovered that her tongue refused its wonted duty. There was a peculiar ache in her throat, and her mouth was dry and furry. She could only look at Hans, who, in turn, looked at her.

Suddenly the silence was broken by a sharp, metallic clang. She screamed, jerking her eyes back to the table. The plate had fallen down. Hans sighed as though awakening from sleep. The clang of the plate had aroused them to life in a new world. The cabin epitomized the new world in which they must thenceforth live and move. The old cabin was gone forever. The horizon of life was totally new and unfamiliar. The unexpected had swept its wizardry over the face of things, changing the perspective, juggling values, and shuffling the real and the unreal into perplexing confusion.

"My God, Hans!" was Edith's first speech.

He did not answer, but stared at her with horror. Slowly his eyes wandered over the room, for the first time taking in its details. Then he put on his cap and started for the door.

"Where are you going?" Edith demanded, in an agony of apprehension.

His hand was on the door knob, and he half

139

turned as he answered, "To dig some graves."

"Don't leave me, Hans, with—" her eyes swept the room—"with this."

"The graves must be dug sometime," he said.

"But you do not know how many," she objected desperately. She noted his indecision, and added, "Besides, I'll go with you and help."

Hans stepped back to the table and mechanically snuffed the candle. Then between them they made the examination. Both Harkey and Dutchy were dead — frightfully dead, because of the close range of the shotgun. Hans refused to go near Dennin, and Edith was forced to conduct this portion of the investigation by herself.

"He isn't dead," she called to Hans.

He walked over and looked down at the murderer.

"What did you say?" Edith demanded, having caught the rumble of inarticulate speech in her husband's throat.

"I said it was a damn shame that he isn't dead," came the reply.

Edith was bending over the body.

"Leave him alone," Hans commanded harshly, in a strange voice.

She looked at him in sudden alarm. He had picked up the shotgun dropped by Dennin and was thrusting in the shells.

"What are you going to do?" she cried, rising swiftly from her bending position.

Hans did not answer, but she saw the shotgun going to his shoulder. She grasped the muzzle with her hand and threw it up.

"Leave me alone!" he cried hoarsely.

He tried to jerk the weapon away from her, but she came in closer and clung to him.

"Hans! Hans! Wake up!" she cried. "Don't be crazy!"

"He killed Dutchy and Harkey!" was her husband's reply; "and I am going to kill him."

"But that is wrong," she objected. "There is the law."

He sneered his incredulity of the law's potency in such a region, but he merely iterated, dispassionately, doggedly, "He killed Dutchy and Harkey."

Long she argued it with him, but the argument was one-sided, for he contented himself with repeating again and again, "He killed Dutchy and Harkey." But she could not escape from her childhood training nor from the blood that was in her. The heritage of law was hers, and right conduct, to her, was the fulfilment of the law. She could see no other righteous course to pursue. Hans's taking the law in his own hands was no more justifiable than Dennin's deed. Two wrongs did not make a right, she contended, and there was

141

only one way to punish Dennin, and that was the legal way arranged by society. At last Hans gave in to her.

"All right," he said. "Have it your own way. And tomorrow or next day look to see him kill you and me."

She shook her head and held out her hand for the shotgun. He started to hand it to her, then hesitated.

"Better let me shoot him," he pleaded.

Again she shook her head, and again he started to pass her the gun, when the door opened, and an Indian, without knocking, came in. A blast of wind and flurry of snow came in with him. They turned and faced him, Hans still holding the shotgun. The intruder took in the scene without a quiver. His eyes embraced the dead and wounded in a sweeping glance. No surprise showed in his face, not even curiosity. Harkey lay at his feet, but he took no notice of him. So far as he was concerned, Harkey's body did not exist.

"Much wind," the Indian remarked by way of salutation. "All well? Very well?"

Hans, still grasping the gun, felt sure that the Indian attributed to him the mangled corpses. He glanced appealingly at his wife.

"Good morning, Negook," she said, her voice

142

betraying her effort. "No, not very well. Much trouble."

"Good-bye, I go now, much hurry," the Indian said, and without semblance of haste, with great deliberation stepping clear of a red pool on the floor, he opened the door and went out.

The man and woman looked at each other.

"He thinks we did it," Hans gasped, "that I did it."

Edith was silent for a space. Then she said, briefly, in a businesslike way:

"Never mind what he thinks. That will come after. At present we have two graves to dig. But first of all, we've got to tie up Dennin so he can't escape."

Hans refused to touch Dennin, but Edith lashed him securely, hand and foot. Then she and Hans went out into the snow. The ground was frozen. It was impervious to a blow of the pick. They first gathered wood, then scraped the snow away and on the frozen surface built a fire. When the fire had burned for an hour, several inches of dirt had thawed. This they shoveled out, and then built a fresh fire. Their descent into the earth progressed at the rate of two or three inches an hour.

It was hard and bitter work. The flurrying snow did not permit the fire to burn any too well, while the wind cut through their clothes and chilled their bodies. They held but little conversation. The wind interfered with speech. Beyond wondering at what could have been Dennin's motive, they remained silent, oppressed by the horror of the tragedy. At one o'clock, looking toward the cabin, Hans announced that he was hungry.

"No, not now, Hans," Edith answered. "I couldn't go back alone into that cabin the way it is, and cook a meal."

At two o'clock Hans volunteered to go with her; but she held him to his work, and four o'clock found the two graves completed. They were shallow, not more than two feet deep, but they would serve the purpose. Night had fallen. Hans got the sled, and the two dead men were dragged through the darkness and storm to their frozen sepulchre. The funeral procession was anything but a pageant. The sled sank deep into the drifted snow and pulled hard. The man and the woman had eaten nothing since the previous day, and were weak from hunger and exhaustion. They had not the strength to resist the wind, and at times its buffets hurled them off their feet. On several occasions the sled was overturned, and they were compelled to reload it with its sombre freight. The last hundred feet to the graves was up a steep slope, and this they took on all fours, like sled dogs, making legs of their arms and thrusting their hands into the snow. Even so, they were twice dragged backward by the weight of the sled, and slid and fell down the hill, the living and the dead, the haul-ropes and the sled, in ghastly entanglement.

"Tomorrow I will put up headboards with their names," Hans said, when the graves were filled in.

Edith was sobbing. A few broken sentences had been all she was capable of in the way of a funeral service, and now her husband was compelled to half-carry her back to the cabin.

Dennin was conscious. He had rolled over and over on the floor in vain efforts to free himself. He watched Hans and Edith with glittering eyes, but made no attempt to speak. Hans still refused to touch the murderer, and sullenly watched Edith drag him across the floor to the men's bunkroom. But try as she would, she could not lift him from the floor into his bunk.

"Better let me shoot him, and we'll have no more trouble," Hans said in final appeal.

Edith shook her head and bent again to her task. To her surprise the body rose easily, and she knew Hans had relented and was helping her. Then came the cleansing of the kitchen. But the floor still shrieked the tragedy, until Hans planed the surface of the stained wood away and with the shavings made a fire in the stove.

The days came and went. There was much of darkness and silence, broken only by the storms and the thunder on the beach of the freezing surf. Hans was obedient to Edith's slightest order. All his splendid initiative had vanished. She had elected to deal with Dennin in her way, and so he left the whole matter in her hands.

The murderer was a constant menace. At all times there was the chance that he might free himself from his bonds, and they were compelled to guard him day and night. The man or the woman sat always beside him, holding the loaded shotgun. At first, Edith tried eight-hour watches, but the continuous strain was too great, and afterwards she and Hans relieved each other every four hours. As they had to sleep, and as the watches extended through the night, their whole waking time was expended in guarding Dennin. They had barely time left over for the preparation of meals and the getting of firewood.

Since Negook's inopportune visit, the Indians had avoided the cabin. Edith sent Hans to their cabins to get them to take Dennin down the coast in a canoe to the nearest white settlement or trading post, but the errand was fruitless. Then Edith went herself and interviewed Negook. He was head

man of the little village, keenly aware of his
responsibility, and he elucidated his policy thor-
oughly in few words.

"It is white man's trouble," he said, "not Siwash trouble. My people help you, then will it be
Siwash trouble too. When white man's trouble and
Siwash trouble come together and make a trouble,
it is a great trouble, beyond understanding and
without end. Trouble no good. My people do no
wrong. What for they help you and have trouble?"

So Edith Nelson went back to the terrible cabin
with its endless alternating four-hour watches.
Sometimes, when it was her turn and she sat by the
prisoner, the loaded shotgun in her lap, her eyes
would close and she would doze. Always she
aroused with a start, snatching up the gun and
swiftly looking at him. These were distinct nervous
shocks, and their effect was not good on her. Such
was her fear of the man, that even though she were
wide awake, if he moved under the bedclothes she
could not repress the start and the quick reach for
the gun.

She was preparing herself for a nervous breakdown, and she knew it. First came a fluttering of
the eyeballs, so that she was compelled to close her
eyes for relief. A little later the eyelids were
afflicted by a nervous twitching that she coud not
control. To add to the strain, she could not forget

147

the tragedy. She remained as close to the horror as on the first morning when the unexpected stalked into the cabin and took possession. In her daily ministrations upon the prisoner she was forced to grit her teeth and steel herself, body and spirit.

Hans was affected differently. He became obsessed by the idea that it was his duty to kill Dennin; and whenever he waited upon the bound man or watched by him, Edith was troubled by the fear that Hans would add another red entry to the cabin's record. Always he cursed Dennin savagely and handled him roughly. Hans tried to conceal his homicidal mania, and he would say to his wife: "By-and-by you will want me to kill him, and then I will not kill him. It would make me sick." But more than once, stealing into the room, when it was her watch off, she would catch the two men glaring ferociously at each other, wild animals the pair of them, in Hans's face the lust to kill, in Dennin's the fierceness and savagery of the cornered rat. "Hans!" she would cry, "wake up!" and he would come to a recollection of himself, startled and shamefaced and unrepentant.

So Hans became another factor in the problem the unexpected had given Edith Nelson to solve. At first it had been merely a question of right conduct in dealing with Dennin, and right conduct, as she conceived it, lay in keeping him a prisoner until he could be turned over for trial before a proper tribunal. But now entered Hans, and she saw that his sanity and his salvation were involved. Nor was she long in discovering that her own strength and endurance had become part of the problem. She was breaking down under the strain. Her left arm had developed involuntary jerkings and twitchings. She spilled her food from her spoon, and could place no reliance on her afflicted arm. She judged it to be a form of St. Vitus's dance, and she feared the extent to which its ravages might go. What if she broke down? And the vision she had of the possible future, when the cabin might contain only Dennin and Hans, was an added horror.

After the third day, Dennin had begun to talk. His first question had been, "What are you going to do with me?" And this question he repeated daily and many times a day. And always Edith replied that he would assuredly be dealt with according to law. In turn, she put a daily question to him — "Why did you do it?" To this he never replied. Also, he received the question with outbursts of anger, raging and straining at the rawhide that bound him and threatening her with what he would do when he got loose, which he said he was sure to do sooner or later. At such times she cocked both triggers of the gun, prepared to meet him with leaden death if he should burst loose, herself trembling and palpitating and dizzy from the tension and shock.

But in time Dennin grew more tractable. It seemed to her that he was growing weary of his unchanging recumbent position. He began to beg and plead to be released. He made wild promises. He would do them no harm. He would himself go down the coast and give himself up to the officers of the law. He would give them his share of the gold. He would go away into the heart of the wilderness, and never again appear in civilization. He would take his own life if she would only free him. His pleading usually culminated in involuntary raving, until it seemed to her that he was passing into a fit; but always she shook her head and denied him the freedom for which he worked himself into a passion.

But the weeks went by, and he continued to grow more tractable. And through it all the weariness was asserting itself more and more. "I am so tired, so tired," he would murmur, rolling his head back and forth on the pillow like a peevish child. At a little later period he began to make impassioned pleas for death, to beg her to kill him, to beg Hans to put him out of his misery so that he might at least rest comfortably.

The situation was fast becoming impossible. Edith's nervousness was increasing, and she knew her breakdown might come any time. She could not even get her proper rest, for she was haunted by the fear that Hans would yield to his mania and kill Dennin while she slept. Though January had already come, months would have to elapse before any trading schooner was even likely to put in to the bay. Also, they had not expected to winter in the cabin, and the food was running low; nor could Hans add to the supply by hunting. They were chained to the cabin by the necessity of guarding their prisoner.

Something must be done, and she knew it. She forced herself to go back into a reconsideration of the problem. She could not shake off the legacy of her race, the law that was of her blood and that had been trained into her. She knew that whatever she did she must do according to the law, and in the long hours of watching, the shotgun on her knees, the murderer restless beside her and the storms thundering without, she made original sociological researches and worked out for herself the evolution of the law. It came to her that the law was nothing more than the judgment and the will of any group of people. It mattered not how large was the group of people. There were little groups, she reasoned, like Switzerland, and there were big groups like the United States. Also, she reasoned, it did not matter how small was the group of people. There might be only ten thousand people in a country, yet their collective judgment and will would be the law of that country. Why, then, could not one thousand people constitute such a group? she asked herself. And if one thousand, why not one hundred? Why not fifty? Why not five? Why not — two?

She was frightened at her own conclusion, and she talked it over with Hans. At first he could not comprehend, and then, when he did, he added convincing evidence. He spoke of miners' meetings, where all the men of a locality came together and made the law and executed the law. There might be only ten or fifteen men altogether, he said, but the will of the majority became the law for the whole ten or fifteen, and whoever violated that will was punished.

Edith saw her way clear at last. Dennin must hang. Hans agreed with her. Between them they constituted the majority of this particular group. It was the group-will that Dennin should be hanged. In the execution of this will Edith strove earnestly to observe the customary forms, but the group was so small that Hans and she had to serve as witnesses, as jury, and as judges — also as executioners. She formally charged Michael Dennin with the murder of Dutchy and Harkey, and the prisoner lay in his bunk and listened to the testimony, first of Hans, and then of Edith. He refused to plead guilty or not guilty, and remained silent when she asked him if he had anything to say in his own defense. She and Hans, without leaving their seats, brought in the jury's verdict of guilty. Then, as judge, she imposed the sentence. Her voice shook, her eyelids twitched, her left arm jerked, but she carried it out.

"Michael Dennin, in three days' time you are to by hanged by the neck until you are dead."

Such was the sentence. The man breathed an unconscious sigh of relief, then laughed defiantly, and said, "Thin I'm thinkin' the damn bunk won't be achin' me back anny more, an' that's a consolation."

With the passing of the sentence a feeling of relief seemed to communicate itself to all of them. Especially was it noticable in Dennin. All sullenness and defiance disappeared, and he talked sociably with his captors, and even with flashes of his old-time wit. Also, he found great satisfaction in Edith's reading to him from the Bible. She read from the New Testament, and he took keen interest in the prodigal son and the thief on the cross.

On the day preceding that set for the execution, when Edith asked her usual question, "Why did you do it?" Dennin answered, "'Tis very simple. I was thinkin'—"

But she hushed him abruptly, asked him to wait, and hurried to Hans's bedside. It was his watch off, and he came out of his sleep, rubbing his eyes and grumbling.

"Go," she told him, "and bring up Negook and one other Indian. Michael's going to confess. Make them come. Take the rifle along and bring them up at the point of it if you have to."

Half an hour later Negook, and his uncle, Hadik-Wan, were ushered into the death chamber. They came unwillingly, Hans with his rifle herding them along.

"Negook," Edith said, "there is to be no trouble for you and your people. Only is it for you to sit and do nothing but listen and understand."

Thus did Michael Dennin, under sentence of death, make public confession of his crime. As he talked, Edith wrote his story down, while the Indians listened, and Hans guarded the door for fear the witnesses might bolt.

He had not been home to the old country for fifteen years, Dennin explained, and it had always been his intention to return with plenty of money and make his old mother comfortable for the rest of her days.

"An' how was I to be doin' it on sixteen hundred?" he demanded. "What I was after wantin' was all the goold, the whole eight thousan'. Thin

I cud go back in style. What ud be aisier, thinks I to myself, than to kill all iv yez, report it at Skagway for an Indian-killin', an' thin pull out for Ireland? An' so I started in to kill all iv yez, but, as Harkey was fond of sayin', I cut out too large a chunk an' fell down on the swallowin' iv it. An' that's me confession. I did me duty to the devil, an' now, God willin', I'll do me duty to God."

"Negook and Hadik-Wan, you have heard the white man's words," Edith said to the Indians. "His words are here on this paper, and it is for you to make a sign, thus, on the paper, so that white men to come after will know that you have heard."

The two Siwashes put crosses opposite their names, received a summons to appear on the morrow with all their tribe for a further witnessing of things, and were allowed to go.

Dennin's hands were released long enough for him to sign the document. Then a silence fell in the room. Hans was restless, and Edith felt uncomfortable. Dennin lay on his back, staring straight up at the moss-chinked roof.

"An' now I'll do me duty to God," he murmured. He turned his head toward Edith. "Read to me," he said, "from the Book"; then added, with a glint of playfulness, "Mayhap 'twill help me to forget the bunk."

The day of the execution broke clear and cold.

The thermometer was down to twenty-five below zero, and a chill wind was blowing which drove the frost through clothes and flesh to the bones. For the first time in many weeks Dennin stood upon his feet. His muscles had remained inactive so long, and he was so out of practice in maintaining an erect position, that he could scarcely stand. He reeled back and forth, staggered, and clutched hold of Edith with his bound hands for support.

"Sure, an' it's dizzy I am," he laughed weakly.

A moment later he said, "An' it's glad I am that it's over with. That damn bunk would iv been the death iv me, I know."

When Edith put his fur cap on his head and proceeded to pull the flaps down over his ears, he laughed and said:

"What are you doin' that for?"

"It's freezing cold outside," she answered.

"An' in tin minutes' time what'll matter a frozen ear or so to poor Michael Dennin?" he asked.

She had nerved herself for the last culminating ordeal, and his remark was like a blow to her self-possession. So far, everything had seemed phantom-like, as in a dream, but the brutal truth of what he had said shocked her eyes wide open to the reality of what was taking place. Nor was her distress unnoticed by the Irishman.

"I'm sorry to be troublin' you with me foolish

spache," he said regretfully. "I mint nothin' by
it. 'Tis a great day for Michael Dennin, an' he's
as gay as a lark."

He broke out in a merry whistle, which quickly
became lugubrious and ceased.

"I'm wishin' there was a priest," he said wist-
fully; then added swiftly, "But Michael Dennin's
too old a campaigner to miss the luxuries when he
hits the trail."

He was so very weak and unused to walking that
when the door opened and he passed outside, the
wind nearly carried him off his feet. Edith and
Hans walked on either side of him and supported
him, the while he cracked jokes and tried to keep
them cheerful, breaking off once long enough to
arrange the forwarding of his share of the gold to
his mother in Ireland.

They climbed a slight hill and came out into an
open space among the trees. Here, circled solemnly
about a barrel that stood on end in the snow, were
Negook and Hadik-Wan, and all the Siwashes down
to the babies and the dogs, come to see the way
of the white man's law. Nearby was an open grave
which Hans had burned into the frozen earth.

Dennin cast a practical eye over the preparations,
noting the grave, the barrel, the thickness of the
rope, and the diameter of the limb over which the
rope was passed.

"Sure, an' I couldn't iv done better meself, Hans, if it'd been for you."

He laughed loudly at his own sally, but Hans's face was frozen into a sullen ghastliness that nothing less than the trump of doom could have broken. Also, Hans was feeling very sick. He had not realized the enormousness of the task of putting a fellow man out of the world. Edith, on the other hand, had realized; but the realization did not make the task any easier. She was filled with doubt as to whether she could hold herself together long enough to finish it. She felt incessant impulses to scream, to shriek, to collapse into the snow, to put her hands over her eyes and turn and run blindly away, into the forest, anywhere, away. It was only by a supreme effort of soul that she was able to keep upright and go on and do what she had to do. And in the midst of it all she was grateful to Dennin for the way he helped her.

"Lind me a hand," he said to Hans, with whose assistance he managed to mount the barrel.

He bent over so that Edith could adjust the rope about his neck. Then he stood upright while Hans drew the rope taut across the overhead branch.

"Michael Dennin, have you anything to say?" Edith asked in a clear voice that shook in spite of her.

Dennin shuffled his feet on the barrel, looked

down bashfully like a man making his maiden speech, and cleared his throat.

"I'm glad it's over with," he said. "You've treated me like a Christian, an' I'm thankin' you hearty for your kindness."

"Then may God receive you, a repentant sinner," she said.

"Ay," he answered, his deep voice as a response to her thin one, "may God receive me, a repintant sinner."

"Good-bye, Michael," she cried, and her voice sounded desperate.

She threw her weight against the barrel, but it did not overturn.

"Hans! Quick! Help me!" she cried faintly.

She could feel her last strength going, and the barrel resisted her. Hans hurried to her, and the barrel went out from under Michael Dennin.

She turned her back, thrusting her fingers into her ears. Then she began to laugh, harshly, sharply, metallically; and Hans was shocked as he had not been shocked through the whole tragedy. Edith Nelson's breakdown had come. Even in her hysteria she knew it, and she was glad that she had been able to hold up under the strain until everything had been accomplished. She reeled toward Hans.

159

"Take me to the cabin, Hans," she managed to articulate.

"And let me rest," she added. "Just let me rest, and rest, and rest."

With Hans's arm around her, supporting her weight and directing her helpless steps, she went off across the snow. But the Indians remained solemnly to watch the working of the white man's law that compelled a man to dance upon the air.

THE WIFE
OF A KING

7

I

ONCE, when the northland was very young,
the social and civic virtues were remarkably
alike for their paucity and their simplicity. When
the burden of domestic duties grew grievous, and
the fireside mood expanded to a constant protest
against its bleak loneliness, the adventurers from
the southland, in lieu of better, paid the stipulated
prices and took unto themselves native wives. It
was a foretaste of paradise to the women, for it
must be confessed that the white rovers gave far
better care and treatment to them than did their
Indian copartners. Of course, the white men themselves were satisfied with such deals, as were also

the Indian men for that matter. Having sold their daughters and sisters for cotton blankets and obsolete rifles, and traded their warm furs for flimsy calico and bad whiskey, the sons of the soil promptly and cheerfully succumbed to quick consumption and other swift diseases correlated with the blessings of a superior civilization.

It was in these days of Arcadian simplicity that Cal Galbraith journeyed through the land and fell sick on the Lower River. It was a refreshing advent in the lives of the good Sisters of the Holy Cross who gave him shelter and medicine, though they little dreamed of the hot elixir infused into his veins by the touch of their soft hands and their gentle ministrations. Cal Galbraith became troubled with strange thoughts, which clamored for attention till he laid eyes on the Mission girl, Madeline. Yet he gave no sign, biding his time patiently. He strengthened with the coming spring, and when the sun rode the heavens in a golden circle, and the joy and throb of life were in all the land, he gathered his still weak body together and departed.

Now Madeline, the Mission girl, was an orphan. Her white father had failed to give a bald-faced grizzly the trail one day, and had died quickly. Then her Indian mother, having no man to fill the winter cache, had tried the hazardous experiment of waiting till the salmon run on fifty pounds of flour and half as many of bacon. After that the baby, Chook-ra, went to live with the good Sisters, and to be thenceforth known by another name.

But Madeline still had kinsfolk, the nearest being a dissolute uncle who outraged his vitals with inordinate quantities of the white man's whiskey. He strove daily to walk with the gods, and incidentally his feet sought shorter trails to the grave. When sober he suffered exquisite torture. He had no conscience. To this ancient vagabond Cal Galbraith duly presented himself, and they consumed many words and much tobacco in the conversation that followed. Promises were also made; and in the end the old heathen took a few pounds of dried salmon and his birchbark canoe, and paddled away to the Mission of the Holy Cross.

It is not given the world to know what promises he made and what lies he told — the Sisters never gossip; but when he returned, upon his swarthy chest there was a brass crucifix, and in his canoe his niece Madeline. That night there was a grand wedding and a *potlach*; so that for two days to follow there was no fishing done by the village. But in the morning Madeline shook the dust of the Lower River from her moccasins, and with her husband, in a poling boat, went to live on the

Upper River in a place known as the Lower Country. And in the years that followed she was a good wife, sharing her husband's hardships and cooking his food. And she kept him in straight trails, till he learned to save his dust and to work mightily. In the end, he struck it rich and built a cabin in Circle City; and his happiness was such that men who came to visit him in his home circle became restless at the sight of it and envied him greatly.

But the northland began to mature, and social amenities to make their appearance. Hitherto, the southland had sent forth its sons; but it now belched forth a new exodus, this time of its daughters. Sisters and wives they were not; but they did not fail to put new ideas in the heads of the men, and to elevate the tone of things in ways peculiarly their own. No more did the squaws gather at the dances, go roaring down the center in the good, old Virginia reels, or make merry with jolly "Dan Tucker." They fell back on their native stoicism, and uncomplainingly watched the rule of their white sisters from the cabins.

Then another exodus came over the mountains from the prolific southland. This time it was of women who became mighty in the land. Their word was law; their law was steel. They frowned upon the Indian wives, while the other women became mild and walked humbly. There were cowards who became ashamed of their ancient covenants with the daughters of the soil, who looked with a new distaste upon their dark-skinned children; but there were also others — men — who remained true and proud of their aboriginal vows. When it became the fashion to divorce the native wives, Cal Galbraith retained his manhood, and in so doing felt the heavy hand of the women who had come last, knew least, but who ruled the land.

One day, the Upper Country, which lies far above Circle City, was pronounced rich. Dog teams carried the news to Salt Water; golden argosies freighted the lure across the North Pacific; wires and cables sang with the tidings; and the world heard for the first time of the Klondike River and the Yukon Country.

Cal Galbraith had lived the years quietly. He had been a good husband to Madeline, and she had blessed him. But somehow discontent fell upon him; he felt vague yearnings for his own kind, for the life he had been shut out from — a general sort of desire, which men sometimes feel, to break out and taste the prime of living. Besides, there drifted down the river wild rumors of the wonderful Eldorado, glowing descriptions of the city of logs and tents, and ludicrous accounts of the *che-cha-quas* who had rushed in and were stampeding the whole country. Circle City was dead. The world had moved on upriver and become a new and most marvelous world.

Cal Galbraith grew restless on the edge of things, and wished to see with his own eyes. So, after the washup, he weighed in a couple of hundred pounds of dust on the Company's big scales, and took a draft for the same on Dawson. Then he put Tom Dixon in charge of his mines, kissed Madeline good-bye, promised to be back before the first mush ice ran, and took passage on an upriver steamer.

Madeline waited — waited through all the three months of daylight. She fed the dogs, gave much of her time to young Cal, watched the short summer fade away and the sun begin its long journey to the south. And she prayed much in the manner of the Sisters of the Holy Cross. The fall came, and with it there was mush ice on the Yukon, and Circle City kings returning to the winter's work at their mines, but no Cal Galbraith. Tom Dixon received a letter, however, for his men sledded up her winter's supply of dry pine. The Company received a letter, for its dogteams filled her cache with their best provisions, and she was told that her credit was limitless.

Through all the ages man has been held the chief instigator of the woes of woman; but in this case the men held their tongues and swore harshly at one of their number who was away, while the women failed utterly to emulate them. So, without needless delay, Madeline heard strange tales of Cal Galbraith's doings; also, of a certain Greek dancer who played with men as children did with bubbles. Now Madeline was an Indian woman, and further, she had no woman friend to whom to go for wise counsel. She prayed and planned by turns, and that night, being quick of resolve and action, she harnessed the dogs, and with young Cal securely lashed to the sled, stole away.

Though the Yukon still ran free, the eddy ice was growing, and each day saw the river dwindling to a slushy thread. Save him who has done the like, no man may know what she endured in traveling a hundred miles on the rim ice; nor may they understand the toil and hardship of breaking the two hundred miles of packed ice which remained after the river froze for good. But Madeline was an Indian woman, so she did these things, and one night there came a knock at Malemute Kid's door. Thereat he fed a team of starving dogs, put a healthy youngster to bed, and turned his attention to an exhausted woman. He removed her icebound moccasins while he listened to her tale, and stuck the point of his knife into her feet that he might see how far they were frozen.

Despite his tremendous virility, Malemute Kid

was possessed of a softer, womanly element, which could win the confidence of a snarling wolf dog or draw confessions from the most wintry heart. Nor did he seek them. Hearts opened to him as spontaneously as flowers to the sun. Even the priest, Father Roubeau, had been known to confess to him, while the men and women of the northland were ever knocking at his door — a door from which the latchstring hung always out. To Madeline, he could do no wrong, make no mistake. She had known him from the time she first cast her lot among the people of her father's race; and to her half-barbaric mind it seemed that in him was centered the wisdom of the ages, that between his vision and the future there could be no intervening veil.

There were false ideals in the land. The social strictures of Dawson were not synonymous with those of the previous era, and the swift maturity of the northland involved much wrong. Malemute Kid was aware of this, and he had Cal Galbraith's measure accurately. He knew a hasty word was the father of much evil; besides, he was minded to teach a great lesson and bring shame upon the man. So Stanley Prince, the young mining expert, was called into the conference the following night, as was also Lucky Jack Harrington and his violin. That same night, Bettles, who owed a great debt to Malemute Kid, harnessed up Cal Galbraith's dogs, lashed Cal Galbraith, junior, to the sled, and slipped away in the dark for Stuart River.

II

"So; one — two — three, one — two — three. Now reverse! No, no! Start up again, Jack. See — this way." Prince executed the movement as one should who has led the cotillion.

"Now; one — two — three, one — two — three. Reverse! Ah! That's better. Try it again. I say, you know, you mustn't look at your feet. One — two — three, one — two — three. Shorter steps! You are not hanging to the gee-pole just now. Try it over. There! that's the way, One — two — three, one — two — three."

Round and round went Prince and Madeline in an interminable waltz. The table and stools had been shoved over against the wall to increase the room. Malemute Kid sat on the bunk, chin to knees, greatly interested. Jack Harrington sat beside him, scraping away on his violin and following the dancers.

It was a unique situation, the undertaking of these three men with the woman. The most pathetic part, perhaps, was the businesslike way in which they went about it. No athlete was ever trained more rigidly for a coming contest, nor wolf dog for the harness, than was she. But they had good material, for Madeline, unlike most women of her race, in her childhood had escaped the carrying of heavy burdens and the toil of the trail. Besides, she was a clean-limbed, willowy creature, possessed of much grace which had not hitherto been realized. It was this grace which the men strove to bring out and knock into shape.

"Trouble with her, she learned to dance all wrong," Prince remarked to the bunk, after having deposited his breathless pupil on the table. "She's quick at picking up; yet I could do better had she never danced a step. But say, Kid, I can't understand this." Prince imitated a peculiar movement of the shoulders and head — a weakness Madeline suffered from in walking.

"Lucky for her she was raised in the Mission," Malemute Kid answered. "Packing, you know — the head strap. Other Indian women have it bad, but she didn't do any packing till after she married, and then only at first. Saw hard lines with that husband of hers. They went through the Forty Mile famine together."

"But can we break it?"

"Don't know. Perhaps long walks with her trainers will make the riffle. Anyway, they'll take it out some, won't they, Madeline?"

The girl nodded assent. If Malemute Kid, who knew all things, said so, why, it was so. That was all there was about it.

She had come over to them, anxious to begin again. Harrington surveyed her in quest of her points, much in the same manner men do horses. It certainly was not disappointing, for he asked with sudden interest, "What did that beggarly uncle of yours get anyway?"

"One rifle, one blanket, twenty bottles of *hooch*. Rifle broke." She said this last scornfully, as though disgusted at how low her maiden-value had been rated.

She spoke fair English, with many pecularities of her husband's speech, but there was still perceptible the Indian accent, the traditional groping after strange gutturals. Even this her instructors had taken in hand, and with no small success, too.

At the next intermission Prince discovered a new predicament.

"I say, Kid," he said, "we're wrong, all wrong. She can't learn in moccasins. Put her feet into slippers, and then onto that waxed floor — phew!"

Madeline raised a foot and regarded her shapeless house moccasin dubiously. In previous winters, both at Circle City and Forty Mile, she had danced many a night away with similar footgear, and there had been nothing the matter. But now — well, if there

171

was anything wrong it was for Malemute Kid to know, not her.

But Malemute Kid did know, and he had a good eye for measures; so he put on his cap and mittens and went down the hill to pay Mrs. Eppingwell a call. Her husband, Clove Eppingwell, was prominent in the community as one of the great government officials. The Kid had noted her slender little foot one night at the Governor's ball. And as he also knew her to be as sensible as she was pretty, it was no task to ask of her a certain small favor.

On his return, Madeline withdrew for a moment to the inner room. When she reappeared Prince was startled.

"By Jove!" he gasped. "Who'd 'a' thought it! The little witch! Why, my sister —"

"Is an English girl," interrupted Malemute Kid, "with an English foot. This girl comes of a small-footed race. Moccasins just broadened her feet healthily, while she did not misshape them by running with the dogs in her childhood."

But this explanation failed utterly to allay Prince's admiration. Harrington's commercial instinct was touched, and as he looked upon the exquisitely turned foot and ankle, there ran through his mind the sordid list: "one rifle, one blanket, twenty bottles of *hooch*."

Madeline was the wife of a king, a king whose

yellow treasure could buy outright a score of fashion's puppets; yet in all her life her feet had known no gear save red-tanned moosehide. At first she looked in awe at the tiny white satin slippers; but she quickly understood the admiration which shone, manlike, in the eyes of the men. Her face flushed with pride. For the moment she was drunken with her woman's loveliness; then she murmured, with increased scorn, "And one rifle broke!"

So the training went on. Every day Malemute Kid led the girl out on long walks devoted to the correction of her carriage and the shortening of her stride. There was little likelihood of her identity being discovered, for Cal Galbraith and the rest of the old-timers were like lost children among the many strangers who had rushed into the land. Besides, the frost of the north has a bitter tongue, and the tender women of the south, to shield their cheeks from its biting caresses, were prone to the use of canvas masks. With faces obscured and bodies lost in squirrel-skin parkas, a mother and daughter, meeting on the trail, would pass as strangers.

The coaching progressed rapidly. At first it had been slow, but later a sudden acceleration had manifested itself. This began from the moment Madeline tried on the white satin slippers, and in so doing, found herself. The pride of her renegade father, apart from any natural self-esteem she might possess, at that instant received its birth. Hitherto, she had deemed herself a woman of an alien breed, of inferior stock, purchased by her lord's favor. Her husband had seemed to her a god, who had lifted her, through no essential virtues on her part, to his own godlike level. But she had never forgotten, even when young Cal was born, that she was not of his people. As he had been a god, so had his womankind been goddesses. She might have contrasted herself with them, but she had never compared. It might have been that familiarity bred contempt. However, be that as it may, she had ultimately come to understand these roving white men, and to weigh them. True, her mind was dark to deliberate analysis, but she yet possessed her woman's clarity of vision in such matters. On the night of the slippers she had measured the bold, open admiration of her three men friends; and for the first time comparison had suggested itself. It was only a foot and an ankle, but — but comparison could not, in the nature of things, cease at that point. She judged herself by their standards till the divinity of her white sisters was shattered. After all, they were only women, and why should she not exalt herself to their place? In doing these things she learned where she lacked, and with the knowledge of her weakness came her strength. And so mightily did she strive that her three trainers often marveled late into the night over the eternal mystery of woman.

In this way Thanksgiving night drew near. At irregular intervals Bettles sent word down from Stuart River regarding the welfare of young Cal. The time of their return was approaching. More than once a casual caller, hearing dance music and the rhythmic pulse of feet, entered only to find Harrington scraping away and the other two beating time or arguing noisily over a mooted step. Madeline was never in evidence, having precipitately fled to the inner room.

On one of these nights Cal Galbraith dropped in. Encouraging news had just come down from Stuart River, and Madeline had surpassed herself — not in walk alone, and carriage and grace, but in womanly roguishness. They had indulged in sharp repartee, and she had defended herself brilliantly; and then, yielding to the intoxication of the moment, and of her own power, she had bullied, and mastered, and wheedled, and patronized them with most astonishing success. And instinctively, involuntarily, they had bowed, not to her beauty, her wisdom, her wit, but to that indefinable something in woman to which man yields yet cannot name. The room was dizzy with sheer delight as she and Prince whirled through the last dance of the evening. Harrington was throwing in inconceivable flourishes, while Malemute Kid, utterly abandoned, had seized the broom and was executing mad gyrations on his own account.

At this instant the door shook with a heavy rap-rap, and their quick glances noted the lifting of the latch. But they had survived similar situations before. Harrington never broke a note. Madeline shot through the waiting door to the inner room. The broom went hurtling under the bunk, and by the time Cal Galbraith and Louis Savoy got their heads in, Malemute Kid and Prince were in each other's arms, wildly schottisching down the room.

As a rule Indian women do not make a practice of fainting on provocation, but Madeline came as near to it as she ever had in her life. For an hour she crouched on the floor, listening to the heavy voices of the men rumbling up and down in mimic thunder. Like familiar chords of childhood melodies, every intonation, every trick of her husband's voice, swept in upon her, fluttering her heart and weakening her knees till she lay half-fainting against the door. It was well she could neither see nor hear when he took his departure.

"When do you expect to go back to Circle City?" Malemute Kid asked simply.

"Haven't thought much about it," he replied. "Don't think till after the ice breaks."

"And Madeline?"

He flushed at the question, and there was a quick droop to his eyes. Malemute Kid could have despised him for that, had he known men less. As it was, his gorge rose against the wives and daughters who had come into the land, and not satisfied with usurping the place of the native women, had put unclean thoughts in the heads of the men and made them ashamed.

"I guess she's all right," the Circle City king answered hastily, and in an apologetic manner. "Tom Dixon's got charge of my interests, you know, and he sees to it that she has everything she wants."

Malemute Kid laid hand upon his arm, and hushed him suddenly. They had stepped out. Overhead, the aurora, a gorgeous wanton, flaunted miracles of color; beneath lay the sleeping town. Far below, a solitary dog gave tongue. The king again began to speak, but the Kid pressed his hand for silence. The sound multiplied. Dog after dog took up the strain till the full-throated chorus swayed the night. To him who hears for the first time this weird song, is told the first and greatest secret of the northland; to him who has heard it often, it is the solemn knell of lost endeavor. It is the plaint of tortured souls, for in it is invested the heritage of the north, the suffering of countless generations — the warning and the requiem to the world's strays.

Cal Galbraith shivered slightly as it died away in half-caught sobs. The Kid read his thoughts openly, and wandered back with him through all the dreary days of famine and disease; and with him was also the patient Madeline, sharing his pains and perils, never doubting, never complaining. His mind's retina vibrated to a score of pictures, stern, clear-cut, and the hand of the past drew back with heavy fingers on his heart. It was the psychological moment. Malemute Kid was half-tempted to play his reserve card and win the game; but the lesson was too mild as yet, and he let it pass. The next instant they had gripped hands, and the king's beaded moccasins were drawing protests from the outraged snow as he crunched down the hill.

Madeline in collapse was another woman to the mischievous creature of an hour before, whose laughter had been so infectious and whose heightened color and flashing eyes had made her teachers for the while forget. Weak and nerveless, she sat in the chair just as she had been dropped there by Prince and Harrington. Malemute Kid frowned. This would never do. When the time of meeting her husband came to hand, she must carry things off with high-handed imperiousness. It was very necessary she should do it after the manner of white women, else the victory would be no victory at all. So he talked to her sternly, without mincing of words, and initiated her into the weaknesses of his own sex, till she came to understand what simpletons men were after all, and why the word of their women was law.

A few days before Thanksgiving night, Malemute Kid made another call on Mrs. Eppingwell. She promptly overhauled her feminine fripperies, paid a protracted visit to the dry-goods department of the P. C. Company, and returned with the Kid to make Madeline's acquaintance. After that came a period such as the cabin had never seen before, and what with cutting, and fitting, and basting, and stitching, and numerous other wonderful and unknowable things, the male conspirators were more often banished the premises than not. At such times the Opera House opened its double storm doors to them. So often did they put their heads together, and so deeply did they drink curious toasts, that the loungers scented unknown creeks of incalculable richness, and it is known that several *che-cha-quas* and at least one old-timer kept their stampeding packs stored behind the bar, ready to hit the trail at a moment's notice.

Mrs. Eppingwell was a woman of capacity; so, when she turned Madeline over to her trainers on Thanksgiving night she was so transformed that they were almost afraid of her. Prince wrapped a Hudson Bay blanket about her with a mock reverence more real than feigned, while Malemute Kid, whose arm she had taken, found it a severe trial to resume his wonted mentorship. Harrington, with the list of purchases still running through his head, dragged along in the rear, nor opened his mouth once all the way down into the town. When they came to the back door of the Opera House they took the blanket from Madeline's shoulders and spread it on the snow. Slipping out of Prince's moccasin's, she stepped upon it in new satin slippers. The masquarade was at its height. She hesitated, but they jerked open the door and shoved her in. Then they ran around to come in by the front entrance.

III

"Where is Freda?" the old-timers questioned, while the *che-cha-quas* were equally energetic in asking who Freda was. The ballroom buzzed with her name. It was on everybody's lips. Grizzled "sourdough boys," day laborers at the mines but proud of their degree, either patronized the spruce-looking tenderfeet and lied eloquently — the "sourdough boys" being specially created to toy with truth — or gave them savage looks of indignation because of their ignorance. Perhaps forty kings of the Upper and Lower Countries were on the floor, each deeming himself hot on the trail and sturdily backing his judgment with the yellow dust of the realm. An assistant was sent to the man at the scales, upon whom had fallen the burden of weighing up the sacks, while several of the gamblers, with the rules of chance at their finger ends, made up alluring books on the field and favorites.

Which was Freda? Time and again the Greek dancer was thought to have been discovered, but each discovery brought panic to the betting ring and a frantic registering of new wagers by those who wished to hedge. Malemute Kid took an interest in the hunt, his advent being hailed uproariously by the revelers who knew him to a man. The Kid had a good eye for the trick of a step, and ear for the lilt of a voice, and his private choice was a marvelous creature who scintillated as the "Aurora Borealis." But the Greek dancer was too subtle for even his penetration. The majority of the gold hunters seemed to have centered their verdict on the "Russian Princess," who was the most graceful in the room, and hence could be no other than Freda Moloof.

During a quadrille a roar of satisfaction went up. She was discovered. At previous balls, in the figure "all hands round," Freda had displayed an inimitable step and variation peculiarly her own. As the figure was called, the "Russian Princess" gave the unique rhythm to limb and body. A chorus of I-told-you-so's shook the squared roof beams, when lo! it was noticed that the "Aurora Borealis" and another mask, the "Spirit of the Pole," were performing the same trick equally well. And when two twin "Sundogs" and a "Frost Queen" followed suit, a second assistant was dispatched to the aid of the man at the scales.

Bettles came off trail in the midst of the excitement, descending upon them in a hurricane of frost. His rimed brows turned to cataracts as he whirled about; his mustache, still frozen, seemed gemmed with diamonds and turned the light in varicolored rays; while the flying feet slipped on the chunks of ice which rattled from his moccasins and German socks. A northland dance is quite an informal affair, the men of the creeks and trails having lost whatever fastidiousness they may have at one time possessed; and only in the high official circles are conventions at all observed. Here, caste carried no significance. Millionaires and paupers, dog drivers and mounted policemen, joined hands with "ladies in the center," and swept around the circle performing most remarkable capers. Primitive in their pleasures, boisterous and rough, they displayed no rudeness, but rather a crude chivalry as genuine as the most polished courtesy.

In his quest for the Greek dancer, Cal Galbraith

managed to get into the same set with the "Russian Princess," toward whom popular suspicion had turned. But by the time he had guided her through one dance, he was willing not only to stake his millions that she was not Freda, but that he had had his arm about her waist before. When or where he could not tell, but the puzzling sense of familiarity so wrought upon him that he turned his attention to the discovery of her identity. Malemute Kid might have aided him instead of occasionally taking the "Princess" for a few turns and talking earnestly to her in low tones. But it was Jack Harrington who paid the "Russian Princess" the most assiduous court. Once he drew Cal Galbraith aside and hazarded wild guesses as to who she was, and explained to him that he was going in to win. This rankled the Circle City king, for man is not by nature monogamous, and he forgot both Madeline and Freda in the new quest.

It was soon noised about that the "Russian Princess" was not Freda Moloof. Interest deepened. Here was a fresh enigma. They knew Freda though they could not find her, but here was somebody they had found and did not know. Even the women could not place her, and they knew every good dancer in the camp. Many took her for one of the official clique, indulging in a silly escapade. Not a few asserted she would disappear before the unmasking. Others were

183

equally positive that she was the woman reporter of the *Kansas City Star*, come to write them up at ninety dollars per column. And the men at the scales worked busily.

At one o'clock every couple took to the floor. The unmasking began amid laughter and delight, like that of carefree children. There was no end of oh's and ah's as mask after mask was lifted. The scintillating "Aurora Borealis" became the brawny woman whose income from washing the community's clothes ran about five hundred a month. The twin "Sundogs" discovered mustaches on their upper lips, and were recognized as brother fraction-kings of Eldorado. In one of the most prominent sets, and the slowest in uncovering, was Cal Galbraith with the "Spirit of the Pole." Opposite him was Jack Harrington and the "Russian Princess." The rest had discovered themselves, yet the Greek dancer was still missing. All eyes were upon the group. Cal Galbraith, in response to their cries, lifted his partner's mask. Freda's wonderful face and brilliant eyes flashed out upon them. A roar went up, to be hushed suddenly in the new and absorbing mystery of the "Russian Princess." Her face was still hidden, and Jack Harrington was struggling with her. The dancers tittered on the tiptoes of expectancy. He crushed her dainty costume roughly, and then — and then the revelers exploded. The joke was on them. They had danced all night with a tabooed native woman.

But those that knew, and they were many, ceased abruptly, and a hush fell upon the room. Cal Galbraith crossed over with great strides, angrily, and spoke to Madeline in polyglot Chinook. But she retained her composure, apparently oblivious to the fact that she was the cynosure of all eyes, and answered him in English. She showed neither fright nor anger, and Malemute Kid chuckled at her well-bred equanimity. The king felt baffled, defeated; his common Siwash wife had passed beyond him.

"Come!" he said finally. "Come on home."

"I beg pardon," she replied; "I have agreed to go to supper with Mr. Harrington. Besides, there's no end of dances promised."

Harrington extended his arm to lead her away. He evinced not the slightest disinclination toward showing his back, but Malemute Kid had by this time edged in closer. The Circle City king was stunned. Twice his hand dropped to his belt, and twice the Kid gathered himself to spring; but the retreating couple passed safely through the supper-room door, where canned oysters were spread at five dollars the plate. The crowd sighed audibly, broke up into couples, and followed them. Freda pouted and went in with Cal Galbraith; but she had a good heart and a sure tongue, and she spoiled his oysters for him. What she said is of no importance, but his face went red and white at intervals, and he swore repeatedly and savagely at himself.

The supper room was filled with a pandemonium of voices, which ceased suddenly as Cal Galbraith stepped over to his wife's table. Since the unmasking considerable weights of dust had been placed as to the outcome. Everybody watched with breathless interest. Harrington's blue eyes were steady, but under the overhanging tablecloth a Smith & Wesson balanced on his knee. Madeline looked up, casually, with little interest.

"May — may I have the next round dance with you?" the king stuttered.

The wife of the king glanced at her card and inclined her head.

THE SON OF
THE WOLF

8

M AN rarely places a proper valuation upon his
womankind, at least not until deprived of
them. He has no conception of the subtle atmos-
phere exhaled by the sex feminine so long as he
bathes in it; but let it be withdrawn, and an ever-
growing void begins to manifest itself in his existence, and he becomes hungry, in a vague sort of
way, for a something so indefinite that he cannot characterize it. If his comrades have no more
experience than himself, they will shake their heads
dubiously and dose him with strong physic. But
the hunger will continue and become stronger; he
will lose interest in the things of his everyday life

and wax morbid; and one day, when the emptiness has become unbearable, a revelation will dawn upon him.

In the Yukon country, when this comes to pass, the man usually provisions a poling boat, if it be summer, and if winter harnesses his dogs, and heads for the southland. A few months later, supposing him to be possessed of a faith in the country, he returns with a wife to share with him in that faith, and incidentally in his hardships. This but serves to show the innate selfishness of man. It also brings us to the trouble of "Scruff" Mackenzie, which occurred in the old days, before the country was stampeded and staked by a tidal wave of *che-cha-quas,* and when the Klondike's only claim to notice was its salmon fisheries.

Scruff Mackenzie bore the earmarks of a frontier birth and a frontier life. His face was stamped with twenty-five years of incessant struggle with nature in her wildest moods — the last two, the wildest and hardest of all, having been spent in groping for the gold which lies in the shadow of the Arctic Circle. When the yearning sickness came upon him he was not surprised, for he was a practical man and had seen other men thus stricken. But he showed no sign of his malady, save that he worked harder. All summer he fought mosquitoes and washed the sure-thing bars of the Stuart River for a double grubstake. Then he floated a raft of house logs down the Yukon to Forty Mile, and put together as comfortable a cabin as any the camp could boast of. In fact, it showed such cosy promise that many men elected to be his partners and to come and live with him. But he crushed their aspirations with rough speech, peculiar for its strength and brevity, and bought a double supply of grub from the trading post.

As has been noted, Scruff Mackenzie was a practical man. If he wanted a thing he usually got it, but in doing so, went no farther out of his way than was necessary. Though a son of toil and hardship, he was averse to a journey of six hundred miles on the ice, a second of two thousand miles on the ocean, and still a third thousand miles or so to his last stamping grounds — all in the mere quest of a wife. Life was too short. So he rounded up his dogs, lashed a curious freight to his sled, and faced across the divide whose westward slopes were drained by the head-reaches of the Tanana.

He was a sturdy traveler, and his wolf dogs could work harder and travel farther on less grub than any other team in the Yukon. Three weeks later he strode into a hunting camp of the Upper Tanana Sticks. They marveled at his temerity; for they had a bad name and had been known to kill white men for as trifling a thing as a sharp axe or a broken rifle. But he went among them single-handed, his bearing being a delicious composite of humility, familiarity, *sang-froid*, and insolence. It required a deft hand and deep knowledge of the barbaric mind effectually to handle such diverse weapons; but he was a past master in the art, knowing when to conciliate and when to threaten with Jove-like wrath.

He first made obeisance to the Chief Thling-Tinneh, presenting him with a couple of pounds of black tea and tobacco, and thereby winning his most cordial regard. Then he mingled with the men and maidens, and that night gave a *potlach*. The snow was beaten down in the form of an oblong, perhaps a hundred feet in length and a quarter as many across. Down the center a long fire was built, while either side was carpeted with spruce boughs. The lodges were forsaken, and the fivescore or so members of the tribe gave tongue to their folk chants in honor of their guest.

Scruff Mackenzie's two years had taught him the not many hundred words of their vocabulary, and he had likewise conquered their deep gutturals, their Japanese idioms, constructions, and honorific and agglutinative particles. So he made oration after their manner, satisfying their instinctive love of poetry with crude flights of eloquence and metaphorical contortions. After Thling-Tinneh and the shaman had responded in kind, he made trifling presents to the menfolk, joined in their singing, and proved an expert in their fifty-two-stick gambling game.

And they smoked his tobacco and were pleased. But among the younger men there was a defiant attitude, a spirit of braggadocio, easily understood by the raw insinuations of the toothless squaws and the giggling of the maidens. They had known few white men, "Sons of the Wolf," but from those few they had learned strange lessons.

Nor had Scruff Mackenzie, for all his seeming carelessness, failed to note these phenomena. In truth, rolled in his sleeping furs, he thought it all over, thought seriously, and emptied many pipes in mapping out a campaign. One maiden only had caught his fancy — none other than Zarinska, daughter to the chief. In features, form, and poise, answering more nearly to the white man's type of beauty, she was almost an anomaly among her tribal sisters. He would possess her, make her his wife, and name her — ah, he would name her Gertrude! Having thus decided, he rolled over on his side and dropped off to sleep, a true son of his all-conquering race.

It was slow work and a stiff game; but Scruff Mackenzie maneuvered cunningly, with an unconcern which served to puzzle the Sticks. He took great care to impress the men that he was a sure shot and a mighty hunter, and the camp rang with his plaudits when he brought down a moose at six hundred yards. Of a night he visited in Chief Thling-Tinneh's lodge of moose and caribou skins, talking big and dispensing tobacco with a lavish hand. Nor did he fail to likewise honor the shaman; for he realized the medicine man's influence with his people, and was anxious to make of him an ally. But that worthy was high and mighty, refused to be propitiated, and was unerringly marked down as a prospective enemy.

Though no opening presented for an interview with Zarinska, Mackenzie stole many a glance to her, giving fair warning of his intent. And well she knew, yet coquettishly surrounded herself with a ring of women whenever the men were away and he had a chance. But he was in no hurry; besides, he knew she could not help but think of him, and a few days of such thought would only better his suit.

At last, one night, when he deemed the time to be ripe, he abruptly left the chief's smoky dwelling and hastened to a neighboring lodge. As usual, she sat with squaws and maidens about her, all engaged in sewing moccasins and beadwork. They laughed at his entrance, and badinage which linked Zarinska to him ran high. But one after the other they were unceremoniously bundled into the outer snow, whence they hurried to spread the tale through all the camp.

His cause was well pleaded, in her tongue, for she did not know his, and at the end of two hours he rose to go.

"So Zarinska will come to the White Man's lodge? Good! I go now to have talk with thy father, for he may not be so minded. And I will give him many tokens; but he must not ask too much. If he say no? Good! Zarinska shall yet come to the White Man's lodge."

He had already lifted the skin flap to depart, when a low exclamation brought him back to the girl's side. She brought herself to her knees on the bearskin mat, her face aglow with true Eve-light, and shyly unbuckled his heavy belt. He looked down, perplexed, suspicious, his ears alert for the slightest sound without. But her next move disarmed his doubt, and he smiled with pleasure. She took from her sewing bag a moosehide sheath, brave with bright beadwork, fantastically designed. She drew his great hunting knife, gazed reverently along the keen edge, half tempted to try it with her thumb, and shot it into place in its new home. Then she slipped the sheath along the belt to its customary resting place, just above the hip.

For all the world, it was like a scene of olden

193

time — a lady and her knight. Mackenzie drew her up full height and swept her red lips with his mustache — the, to her, foreign caress of the Wolf. It was a meeting of the stone age and the steel.

There was a thrill of excitement in the air as Scruff Mackenzie, a bulky bundle under his arm, threw open the flap of Thling-Tinneh's tent. Children were running about in the open, dragging dry wood to the scene of the *potlach*, a babble of women's voices was growing in intensity, the young men were consulting in sullen groups, while from the shaman's lodge rose the eerie sounds of an incantation.

The chief was alone with his blear-eyed wife, but a glance sufficed to tell Mackenzie that the news was already old. So he plunged at once into the business, shifting the beaded sheath prominently to the fore as advertisement of the betrothal.

"O Thling-Tinneh, mighty chief of the Sticks and the land of the Tanana, ruler of the salmon and the bear, the moose and the caribou! The White Man is before thee with a great purpose. Many moons has his lodge been empty, and he is lonely. And his heart has eaten itself in silence, and grown hungry for a woman to sit beside him in his lodge, to meet him from the hunt with warm fire and good food. He has heard strange things, the patter of baby moccasins and the sound of children's voices. And one night a vision came upon him, and he beheld the Raven, who is thy father, the great Raven, who is the father of all the Sticks. And the Raven spake to the lonely White Man, saying: 'Bind thou thy moccasins upon thee, and gird thy snowshoes on, and lash thy sled with food for many sleeps and fine tokens for the Chief Thling-Tinneh. For thou shalt turn thy face to where the midspring sun is wont to sink below the land, and journey to this great chief's hunting grounds. There thou shalt make big presents, and Thling-Tinneh, who is my son, shall become to thee as a father. In his lodge there is a maiden into whom I breathed the breath of life for thee. This maiden shalt thou take to wife.'

"O Chief, thus spake the great Raven; thus do I lay many presents at thy feet; thus am I come to take thy daughter!"

The old man drew his furs about him with crude consciousness of royalty, but delayed reply while a youngster crept in, delivered a quick message to appear before the council, and was gone.

"O White Man, whom we have named Moose-Killer, also known as the Wolf, and the Son of the Wolf! We know thou comest of a mighty race; we are proud to have thee our *potlach* guest; but the

195

king salmon does not mate with the dog salmon, nor the Raven with the Wolf."

"Not so!" cried Mackenzie. "The daughters of the Raven have I met in the camps of the Wolf — the squaw of Mortimer, the squaw of Tregidgo, the squaw of Barnaby, who came two ice-runs back, and I have heard of other squaws, though my eyes beheld them not."

"Son, your words are true; but it were evil mating, like the water with the sand, like the snowflake with the sun. But meet you one Mason and his squaw? No? He came ten ice-runs ago — the first of all the Wolves. And with him there was a mighty man, straight as a willow shoot, and tall; strong as the bald-faced grizzly, with a heart like the full summer moon; his —"

"Oh!" interrupted Mackenzie, recognizing the well-known northland figure — "Malemute Kid!"

"The same — a mighty man. But saw you aught of the squaw? She was full sister to Zarinska."

"Nay, Chief, but I have heard. Mason — far, far to the north, a spruce tree, heavy with years, crushed out his life beneath. But his love was great, and he had much gold. With this, and her boy, she journeyed countless sleeps toward the winter's noonday sun, and there she yet lives — no biting frost, no snow, no summer's midnight sun, no winter's noonday night."

A second messenger interrupted with imperative summons from the council. As Mackenzie threw him into the snow, he caught a glimpse of the swaying forms before the council fire, heard the deep basses of the men in rhythmic chant, and knew the shaman was fanning the anger of his people. Time pressed. He turned upon the chief.

"Come! I wish thy child. And now. See! Here are tobacco, tea, many cups of sugar, warm blankets, handkerchiefs, both good and large; and here, a true rifle, with many bullets and much powder."

"Nay," replied the old man, struggling against the great wealth spread before him. "Even now are my people come together. They will not have this marriage."

"But thou art chief."

"Yet do my young men rage because the Wolves have taken their maidens so that they may not marry."

"Listen, O Thling-Tinneh! Ere the night has passed into the day, the Wolf shall face his dogs to the Mountains of the East and fare forth to the Country of the Yukon. And Zarinska shall break trail for his dogs."

"And ere the night has gained its middle, my young men may fling to the dogs the flesh of the Wolf, and his bones be scattered in the snow till the springtime lay them bare."

197

It was threat and counterthreat. Mackenzie's bronzed face flushed darkly. He raised his voice. The old squaw, who till now had sat an impassive spectator, made to creep by him for the door. The song of the men broke suddenly, and there was a hubbub of many voices as he whirled the old woman roughly to her couch of skins.

"Again I cry — listen, O Thling-Tinneh! The Wolf dies with teeth fast-locked, and with him there shall sleep ten of thy strongest men — men who are needed, for the hunting is but begun, and the fishing is not many moons away. And again, of what profit should I die? I know the custom of thy people; thy share of my wealth shall be very small. Grant me thy child, and it shall all be thine. And yet again, my brothers will come, and they are many, and their maws are never filled; and the daughters of the Raven shall bear children in the lodges of the Wolf. My people are greater than thy people. It is destiny. Grant, and all this wealth is thine."

Moccasins were crunching the snow without. Mackenzie threw his rifle to cock, and loosened the twin Colts in his belt.

"Grant, O Chief!"

"And yet will my people say no."

"Grant, and the wealth is thine. Then shall I deal with thy people after."

"The Wolf will have it so. I will take his tokens — but I would warn him."

Mackenzie passed over the goods, taking care to clog the rifle's ejector, and capping the bargain with a kaleidoscopic silk kerchief. The shaman and half a dozen young braves entered, but he shouldered boldly among them and passed out.

"Pack!" was his laconic greeting to Zarinska as he passed her lodge and hurried to harness his dogs. A few minutes later he swept into the council at the head of the team, the woman by his side. He took his place at the upper end of the oblong, by the side of the chief. To his left, a step to the rear, he stationed Zarinska — her proper place. Besides, the time was ripe for mischief, and there was need to guard his back.

On either side, the men crouched to the fire, their voices lifted in a folk chant out of the forgotten past. Full of strange, halting cadences and haunting recurrences, it was not beautiful. "Fearful" may inadequately express it. At the lower end, under the eye of the shaman, danced half a score of women. Stern were his reproofs to those who did not wholly abandon themselves to the ecstasy of the rite. Half-hidden in their heavy masses of raven hair, all disheveled and falling to their waists, they slowly swayed to and fro, their forms rippling to an ever-changing rhythm.

It was a weird scene; an anachronism. To the south, the nineteenth century was reeling off the few years of its last decade; here flourished man primeval, a shade removed from the prehistoric cave dweller, a forgotten fragment of the elder world. The tawny wolf dogs sat between their skin-clad masters or fought for room, the firelight cast backward from their red eyes and slavered fangs. The woods, in ghostly shroud, slept on unheeding. The White Silence, for the moment driven to the rimming forest, seemed ever crushing inward; the stars danced with great leaps, as is their wont in the time of the Great Cold; while the Spirits of the Pole trailed their robes of glory athwart the heavens.

Scruff Mackenzie dimly realized the wild grandeur of the setting as his eyes ranged down the fur-fringed sides in quest of missing faces. They rested for a moment on a newborn babe, suckling at its mother's naked breast. It was forty below — seventy and odd degrees of frost. He thought of the tender women of his own race, and smiled grimly. Yet from the loins of some such tender woman had he sprung with a kingly inheritance — an inheritance which gave to him his dominance over the land and sea, over the animals and the peoples of all the zones. Singlehanded against five-score, girt by the Arctic winter, far from his own, he felt the prompting of his heritage, the desire to possess, the wild danger-love, the thrill of battle, the power to conquer or to die.

The singing and the dancing ceased, and the shaman flared up in rude eloquence. Through the sinuosities of their vast mythology, he worked cunningly upon the credulity of his people. The case was strong. Opposing the creative principles as embodied in the Crow and the Raven, he stigmatized Mackenzie as the Wolf, the fighting and the destructive principle. Not only was the combat of these forces spiritual, but men fought, each to his totem. They were the children of Jelchs, the Raven, the Promethean fire-bringer; Mackenzie was the child of the Wolf, or, in other words, the Devil. For them to bring a truce to this perpetual warfare, to marry their daughters to the arch-enemy, were treason and blasphemy of the highest order. No phrase was harsh nor figure vile enough in branding Mackenzie as a sneaking interloper and emissary of Satan. There was a subdued, savage roar in the deep chests of his listeners as he took the swing of his peroration.

"Ay, my brothers, Jelchs is all-powerful! Did he not bring heaven-born fire that we might be warm? Did he not draw the sun, moon, and stars from their holes that we might see? Did he not teach us that we might fight the Spirits of Famine and of Frost?

But now Jelchs is angry with his children, and they are grown to a handful, and he will not help. For they have forgotten him, and done evil things, and trod bad trails, and taken his enemies into their lodges to sit by their fires. And the Raven is sorrowful at the wickedness of his children; but when they shall rise up and show they have come back, he will come out of the darkness to aid them. O brothers! The Fire-Bringer has whispered messages to thy shaman; the same shall ye hear. Let the young men take the young women to their lodges; let them fly at the throat of the Wolf; let them be undying in their enmity! Then shall their women become fruitful, and they shall multiply into a mighty people! And the Raven shall lead great tribes of their fathers and their fathers' fathers from out of the north; and they shall beat back the Wolves till they are as last year's campfires; and they shall again come to rule over all the land! 'Tis the message of Jelchs, the Raven."

This foreshadowing of the Messiah's coming brought a hoarse howl from the Sticks as they leaped to their feet. Mackenzie slipped the thumbs of his mittens, and waited. There was a clamor for the Fox, not to be stilled till one of the young men stepped forward to speak.

"Brothers! The shaman has spoken wisely. The Wolves have taken our women, and our men are childless. We are grown to a handful. The Wolves have taken our warm furs, and given for them evil spirits which dwell in bottles, and clothes which come not from the beaver or the lynx, but are made from the grass. And they are not warm, and our men die of strange sicknesses. I, the Fox, have taken no woman to wife; and why? Twice have the maidens which pleased me gone to the camps of the Wolf. Even now have I laid by skins of the beaver, of the moose, of the caribou, that I might win favor in the eyes of Thling-Tinneh, that I might marry Zarinska, his daughter. Even now are her snowshoes bound to her feet, ready to break trail for the dogs of the Wolf. Nor do I speak for myself alone. As I have done, so has the Bear. He, too, had fain been the father of her children, and many skins has he cured thereto. I speak for all the young men who know not wives. The Wolves are ever hungry. Always do they take the choice meat at the killing. To the Ravens are left the leavings.

"There is Gugklal!" he cried, brutally pointing out one of the women, who was a cripple. "Her legs are bent like the ribs of a birch canoe. She cannot gather wood nor carry the meat of the hunters. Did the Wolves choose her?"

"Ail ai!" vociferated his tribesmen.

"There is Moyri, whose eyes are crossed by the

203

Evil Spirit. Even the babes are affrighted when they gaze upon her, and it is said the bald-face gives her the trail. Was she chosen?"

Again the cruel applause rang out.

"And there sits Pischet. She does not hearken to my words. Never has she heard the cry of the chit-chat, the voice of her husband, the babble of her child. She lives in the White Silence. Cared the Wolves aught for her? No! Theirs is the choice of the kill; ours is the leavings.

"Brothers, it shall not be! No more shall the Wolves slink among our campfires. The time is come."

A great streamer of fire, the aurora borealis, purple, green, and yellow, shot across the zenith, bridging horizon to horizon. With head thrown back and arms extended, he swayed to his climax.

"Behold! The spirits of our fathers have arisen and great deeds are afoot this night!"

He stepped back, and another young man somewhat diffidently came forward, pushed on by his comrades. He towered a full head above them, his broad chest definantly bared to the frost. He swung tentatively from one foot to the other. Words halted upon his tongue, and he was ill at ease. His face was horrible to look upon, for it had at one time been half torn away by some terrific blow. At last he struck his breast with his clenched fist, drawing sound as from a drum, and his voice rumbled forth as the surf from an ocean cavern.

"I am the Bear — the Silver-Tip and the Son of the Silver-Tip! When my voice was yet as a girl's, I slew the lynx, the moose, and the caribou; when it whistled like the wolverines from under a cache, I crossed the Mountains of the South and slew three of the White Rivers; when it became as the roar of the Chinook, I met the bald-faced grizzly, but gave no trail."

At this he paused, his hand significantly sweeping across his hideous scars.

"I am not as the Fox. My tongue is frozen like the river. I cannot make great talk. My words are few. The Fox says great deeds are afoot this night. Good! Talk flows from his tongue like the freshets of the spring, but he is chary of deeds. This night shall I do battle with the Wolf. I shall slay him, and Zarinska shall sit by my fire. The Bear has spoken."

Though pandemonium raged about him, Scruff Mackenzie held his ground. Aware how useless was the rifle at close quarters, he slipped both holsters to the fore, ready for action, and drew his mittens till his hands were barely shielded by the elbow gauntlets. He knew there was no hope in attack *en masse*, but true to his boast, was prepared to die with teeth fast-locked. But the Bear restrained his comrades, beating back the more impetuous with his terrible fist. As the tumult began to die away, Mackenzie shot a glance in the direction of Zarinska. It was a superb picture. She was leaning forward on her snowshoes, lips apart and nostrils quivering, like a tigress about to spring. Her great black eyes were fixed upon her tribesmen, in fear and in defiance. So extreme the tension, she had forgotten to breathe. With one hand pressed spasmodically against her breast and the other as tightly gripped about the dog whip, she was as turned to stone. Even as he looked, relief came to her. Her muscles loosened; with a heavy sigh she settled back, giving him a look of more than love.

Thling-Tinneh was trying to speak, but his people drowned his voice. Then Mackenzie strode forward. The Fox opened mouth to a piercing yell, but so savagely did Mackenzie whirl upon him that he shrank back, his larynx all agurgle with suppressed sound. His discomfiture was greeted with roars of laughter, and served to soothe his fellows to a listening mood.

"Brothers! The White Man, whom ye have chosen to call the Wolf, came among you with fair words. He was not like the Innuit; he spoke not lies. He came as a friend, as one who would be a brother. But your men have had their say, and the time for soft words is past. First, I will tell you that the

shaman has an evil tongue and is a false prophet,
that the messages he spake are not those of the
Fire-Bringer. His ears are locked to the voice of
the Raven, and out of his own head he weaves cunning fancies, and he has made fools of you. He has
no power. When the dogs were killed and eaten,
and your stomachs were heavy with untanned hide
and strips of moccasins; when the old men died,
and the old women died, and the babes at the
dry dugs of the mothers died; when the land was
dark, and ye perished as do the salmon in the fall;
ay, when the famine was upon you, did the shaman
bring reward to your hunters? Did the shaman put
meat in your bellies? Again I say, the shaman is
without power. Thus! I spit upon his face!"

Though taken aback by the sacrilege, there was
no uproar. Some of the women were even frightened, but among the men there was an uplifting,
as though in preparation or anticipation of the
miracle. All eyes were turned upon the two central
figures. The priest realized the crucial moment, felt
his power tottering, opened his mouth in denun-
ciation, but fled backward before the truculent advance, upraised fist, and flashing eyes of Mackenzie.
He sneered and resumed.

"Was I stricken dead? Did the lightning burn
me? Did the stars fall from the sky and crush me?
Pish! I have done with the dog. Now will I tell you

of my people, who are the mightiest of all the peoples, who rule in all the lands. At first we hunt as I hunt, alone. After that we hunt in packs; and at last, like the caribou-run, we sweep across all the land. Those whom we take into our lodges live; those who will not come die. Zarinska is a comely maiden, full and strong, fit to become the mother of Wolves. Though I die, such shall she become; for my brothers are many, and they will follow the scent of my dogs. Listen to the Law of the Wolf: *Whoso taketh the life of one Wolf, the forfeit shall ten of his people pay.* In many lands has the price been paid; in many lands shall it yet be paid.

"Now will I deal with the Fox and the Bear. It seems they have cast eyes upon the maiden. So? Behold, I have bought her! Thling-Tinneh leans upon the rifle; the goods of purchase are by his fire. Yet will I be fair to the young men. To the Fox, whose tongue is dry with many words, will I give of tobacco five long plugs. Thus will his mouth be wetted that he may make much noise in the council. But to the Bear, of whom I am well proud, will I give of blankets two; of flour, twenty cups; of tobacco, double that of the Fox; and if he fare with me over the Mountains of the East, then will I give him a rifle, mate to Thling-Tinneh's. If not? Good! The Wolf is weary of speech. Yet once again will he say the Law: *Whoso taketh the life of one Wolf, the forfeit shall ten of his people pay."*

Mackenzie smiled as he stepped back to his old position, but at heart he was full of trouble. The night was yet dark. The girl came to his side, and he listened closely as she told of the Bear's battle tricks with the knife.

The decision was for war. In a trice, scores of moccasins were widening the space of beaten snow by the fire. There was much chatter about the seeming defeat of the shaman; some averred he had but withheld his power, while others conned past events and agreed with the Wolf. The Bear came to the center of the battleground, a long naked hunting knife of Russian make in his hand. The Fox called attention to Mackenzie's revolvers; so he stripped his belt, buckling it about Zarinska, into whose hands he also entrusted his rifle. She shook her head that she could not shoot — small chance had a woman to handle such precious things.

"Then, if danger come by my back, cry aloud, 'My husband!' No; thus, 'My husband!' "

He laughed as she repeated it, pinched her cheek, and re-entered the circle. Not only in reach and stature had the Bear the advantage of him, but his blade was longer by a good two inches. Scruff Mackenzie had looked into the eyes of men before, and he knew it was a man who stood against him;

yet he quickened to the glint of light on the steel, to the dominant pulse of his race.

Time and again he was forced to the edge of the fire or the deep snow, and time and again, with the foot tactics of the pugilist, he worked back to the center. Not a voice was lifted in encouragement, while his antagonist was heartened with applause, suggestions, and warnings. But his teeth only shut the tighter as the knives clashed together, and he thrust or eluded with a coolness born of conscious strength. At first he felt compassion for his enemy; but this fled before the primal instinct of life, which in turn gave way to the lust of slaughter. The ten thousand years of culture fell from him, and he was a cave dweller, doing battle for his female.

Twice he pricked the Bear, getting away unscathed; but the third time caught, and to save himself, free hands closed on fighting hands, and they came together. Then did he realize the tremendous strength of his opponent. His muscles were knotted in painful lumps, and cords and tendons threatened to snap with the strain; yet nearer and nearer came the Russian steel. He tried to break away, but only weakened himself. The fur-clad circle closed in, certain of and anxious to see the final stroke. But with a wrestler's trick, swinging partly to the side, he struck at his adversary with his head. Involuntarily the Bear leaned back, disturbing his center of gravity. Simultaneous with this, Mackenzie tripped properly and threw his whole weight forward, hurling him clear through the circle into the deep snow. The Bear floundered out and came back full tilt.

"O my husband!" Zarinska's voice rang out, vibrant with danger.

To the twang of a bowstring, Mackenzie swept low to the ground, and a bone-barbed arrow passed over him into the breast of the Bear, whose momentum carried him over his crouching foe. The next instant Mackenzie was up and about. The Bear lay motionless, but across the fire was the shaman, drawing a second arrow.

Mackenzie's knife leaped short in the air. He caught the heavy blade by the point. There was a flash of light as it spanned the fire. Then the shaman, the hilt alone appearing without his throat, swayed a moment and pitched forward into the glowing embers.

Click! click! — the Fox had possessed himself of Thling-Tinneh's rifle and was vainly trying to throw a shell into place. But he dropped it at the sound of Mackenzie's laughter.

"So the Fox has not learned the way of the plaything? He is yet a woman. Come! Bring it, that I may show thee!"

The Fox hesitated.

"Come, I say!"

He slouched forward like a beaten cur.

"Thus, and thus; so the thing is done." A shell flew into place and the trigger was at cock as Mackenzie brought it to shoulder.

"The Fox has said great deeds were afoot this night, and he spoke true. There have been great deeds, yet least among them were those of the Fox. Is he still intent to take Zarinska to his lodge? Is he minded to tread the trail already broken by the shaman and the Bear? No? Good!"

Mackenzie turned contemptuously and drew his knife from the priest's throat.

"Are any of the young men so minded? If so, the Wolf will take them by two and three till none are left. No? Good! Thling-Tinneh, I now give thee this rifle a second time. If in the days to come thou shouldst journey to the Country of the Yukon, know thou that there shall always be a place and much food by the fire of the Wolf. The night is now passing into the day. I go, but I may come again. And for the last time, remember the Law of the Wolf!"

He was supernatural in their sight as he rejoined Zarinska. She took her place at the head of the team, and the dogs swung into motion. A few moments later they were swallowed up by the ghostly forest. Till now Mackenzie had waited; he slipped into his snowshoes to follow.

"Has the Wolf forgotten the five long plugs?"

Mackenzie turned upon the Fox angrily; then the humor of it struck him.

"I will give thee one short plug."

"As the Wolf sees fit," meekly responded the Fox, stretching out his hand.

LOVE OF LIFE

9

"This out of all will remain —
  They have lived and have tossed:
So much of the game will be gain,
  Though the gold of the dice has been lost."

THEY limped painfully down the bank, and
  once the foremost of the two men staggered
among the rough-strewn rocks. They were tired
and weak, and their faces had the drawn expression
of patience which comes of hardship long endured.
They were heavily burdened with blanket packs
which were strapped to their shoulders. Head
straps, passing across the forehead, helped support

these packs. Each man carried a rifle. They walked in a stooped posture, the shoulders well forward, the head still farther forward, the eyes bent upon the ground.

"I wish we had just about two of them cartridges that's layin' in that cache of ourn," said the second man.

His voice was utterly and drearily expressionless. He spoke without enthusiasm; and the first man, limping into the milky stream that foamed over the rocks, vouchsafed no reply.

The other man followed at his heels. They did not remove their footgear, though the water was icy cold — so cold that their ankles ached and their feet went numb. In places the water dashed against their knees, and both men staggered for footing.

The man who followed slipped on a smooth boulder, nearly fell, but recovered himself with a violent effort, at the same time uttering a sharp exclamation of pain. He seemed faint and dizzy and put out his free hand while he reeled, as though seeking support against the air. When he had steadied himself he stepped forward, but reeled again and nearly fell. Then he stood still and looked at the other man, who had never turned his head.

The man stood still for fully a minute, as though debating with himself. Then he called out:

"I say, Bill, I've sprained my ankle."

Bill staggered on through the milky water. He did not look around. The man watched him go, and though his face was expressionless as ever, his eyes were like the eyes of a wounded deer.

The other man limped up the farther bank and continued straight on without looking back. The man in the stream watched him. His lips trembled a little, so that the rough thatch of brown hair which covered them was visibly agitated. His tongue even strayed out to moisten them.

"Bill!" he cried out.

It was a pleading cry of a strong man in distress, but Bill's head did not turn. The man watched him go, limping grotesquely and lurching forward with stammering gait up the slow slope toward the soft skyline of the low-lying hill. He watched him go till he passed over the crest and disappeared. Then he turned his gaze and slowly took in the circle of the world that remained to him now that Bill was gone.

Near the horizon the sun was smoldering dimly, almost obscured by formless mists and vapors, which gave an impression of mass and density without outline or tangibility. The man pulled out his watch, the while resting his weight on one leg. It was four o'clock, and as the season was near the last of July or first of August — he did not know

the precise date within a week or two — he knew
that the sun roughly marked the northwest. He
looked to the south and knew that somewhere beyond those bleak hills lay the Great Bear Lake; also,
he knew that in that direction the Arctic Circle
cut its forbidding way across the Canadian Barrens.
This stream in which he stood was a feeder to the
Coppermine River, which in turn flowed north and
emptied into Coronation Gulf and the Arctic Ocean.
He had never been there, but he had seen it on
a Hudson Bay Company chart.

Again his gaze completed the circle of the world
about him. It was not a heartening spectacle. Everywhere was soft skyline. The hills were all low-lying.
There were no trees, no shrubs, no grasses — nothing but a tremendous and terrible desolation that
sent fear swiftly dawning into his eyes.

"Bill!" he whispered, once and twice; "Bill!"

He cowered in the midst of the milky water, as
though the vastness were pressing in upon him
with overwhelming force, brutally crushing him
with its complacent awfulness. He began to shake
as with an ague fit, till the gun fell from his hand
with a splash. This served to rouse him. He fought
with his fear and pulled himself together, groping
in the water and recovering the weapon. He hitched
his pack farther over on his left shoulder, so as to
take a portion of its weight from the injured ankle.

Then he proceeded slowly and carefully, wincing with pain, to the bank.

He did not stop. With a desperation that was madness, unmindful of the pain, he hurried up the slope to the crest of the hill over which his comrade had disappeared — more grotesque and comical by far than that limping, jerking comrade. But at the crest he saw a shallow valley, empty of life. He fought with his fear again, overcame it, hitched the pack still farther over on his left shoulder, and lurched on down the slope.

The bottom of the valley was soggy with water, which the thick moss held spongelike close to the surface. This water squirted out from under his feet at every step, and each time he lifted a foot the action culminated in a sucking sound as the wet moss reluctantly released its grip. He picked his way from muskeg to muskeg, and followed the other man's footsteps along and across the rocky ledges which thrust like islets through the sea of moss.

Though alone, he was not lost. Farther on he knew he would come to where dead spruce and fir, very small and weazened, bordered the shore of a little lake — the *titchin-nichilie*, in the tongue of the country — the "land of little sticks." And into that lake flowed a small stream, the water of which was not milky. There was rush-grass on that stream

— this he remembered well — but no timber, and he would follow it till its first trickle ceased at a divide. He would cross this divide to the first trickle of another stream flowing to the west, which he would follow until it emptied into the river Dease, and here he would find a cache under an upturned canoe and piled over with many rocks. And in this cache would be ammunition for his empty gun, fishhooks and lines, a small net — all the utilities for the killing and snaring of food. Also, he would find flour — not much — a piece of bacon, and some beans.

Bill would be waiting for him there, and they would paddle away south down the Dease to the Great Bear Lake. And south across the lake they would go, ever south, till they gained the Mackenzie. And south, still south, they would go, while the winter raced vainly after them, and the ice formed in the eddies, and the days grew chill and crisp, south to some warm Hudson Bay Company post, where timber grew tall and generous and there was grub without end.

These were the thoughts of the man as he strove onward. But hard as he strove with his body, he strove equally hard with his mind, trying to think that Bill had not deserted him, that Bill would surely wait for him at the cache. He was compelled to think this thought, or else there would not be any use to strive, and he would have lain down and died. And as the dim ball of the sun sank slowly into the northwest he covered every inch — and many times — of his and Bill's flight south before the downcoming winter. And he conned the grub of the cache and the grub of the Hudson Bay Company post over and over again. He had not eaten for two days; for a far longer time he had not had all he wanted to eat. Often he stooped and picked pale muskeg berries, put them into his mouth, and chewed and swallowed them. A muskeg berry is a bit of seed enclosed in a bit of water. In the mouth the water melts away and the seed chews sharp and bitter. The man knew there was no nourishment in the berries, but he chewed them patiently with a hope greater than knowledge and defying experience.

At nine o'clock he stubbed his toe on a rocky ledge, and from sheer weariness and weakness staggered and fell. He lay for some time, without movement, on his side. Then he slipped out of the packstraps and clumsily dragged himself into a sitting posture. It was not yet dark, and in the lingering twilight he groped about among the rocks for shreds of dry moss. When he had gathered a heap he built a fire — a smoldering, smudgy fire — and put a tin pot of water on to boil.

He unwrapped his pack and the first thing he

did was to count his matches. There were sixty-seven. He counted them three times to make sure. He divided them into several portions, wrapping them in oil paper, disposing of one bunch in his empty tobacco pouch, of another bunch in the inside band of his battered hat, of a third bunch under his shirt on his chest. This accomplished, a panic came upon him, and he unwrapped them all and counted them again. There were still sixty-seven.

He dried his wet footgear by the fire. The moccasins were in soggy shreds. The blanket socks were worn through in places, and his feet were raw and bleeding. His ankle was throbbing, and he gave it an examination. It had swollen to the size of his knee. He tore a long strip from one of his two blankets and bound the ankle tightly. He tore other strips and bound them about his feet to serve for both moccasins and socks. Then he drank the pot of water, steaming hot, wound his watch, and crawled between his blankets.

He slept like a dead man. The brief darkness around midnight came and went. The sun arose in the northeast — at least the day dawned in that quarter, for the sun was hidden by gray clouds.

At six o'clock he awoke, quietly lying on his back. He gazed straight up into the gray sky and knew that he was hungry. As he rolled over on his elbow he was startled by a loud snort, and saw a bull caribou regarding him with alert curiosity. The animal was not more than fifty feet away, and instantly into the man's mind leaped the vision and the savor of a caribou steak sizzling and frying over a fire. Mechanically he reached for the empty gun, drew a bead, and pulled the trigger. The bull snorted and leaped away, his hoofs rattling and clattering as he fled across the ledges.

The man cursed and flung the empty gun from him. He groaned aloud as he started to drag himself to his feet. It was a slow and arduous task. His joints were like rusty hinges. They worked harshly in their sockets, with much friction, and each bending or unbending was accomplished only through a sheer exertion of will. When he finally gained his feet, another minute or so was consumed in straightening up, so that he could stand erect as a man should stand.

He crawled up a small knoll and surveyed the prospect. There were no trees, no bushes, nothing but a gray sea of moss scarcely diversified by gray rocks, gray lakelets, and gray streamlets. The sky was gray. There was no sun nor hint of sun. He had no idea of north, and he had forgotten the way he had come to this spot the night before. But he was not lost. He knew that. Soon he would come to the land of the little sticks. He felt that it lay off to the left somewhere, not far — possibly just over the next low hill.

He went back to put his pack into shape for traveling. He assured himself of the existence of his three separate parcels of matches, though he did not stop to count them. But he did linger, debating, over a squat moose-hide sack. It was not large. He could hide it under his two hands. He knew that it weighed fifteen pounds — as much as all the rest of the pack — and it worried him. He finally set it to one side and proceeded to roll the pack. He paused to gaze at the squat moose-hide sack. He picked it up hastily with a defiant glance about him, as though the desolation were trying to rob him of it; and when he rose to his feet to stagger on into the day, it was included in the pack on his back.

He bore away to the left, stopping now and again to eat muskeg berries. His ankle had stiffened, his limp was more pronounced, but the pain of it was as nothing compared with the pain of his stomach. The hunger pangs were sharp. They gnawed and gnawed until he could not keep his mind steady on the course he must pursue to gain the land of little sticks. The muskeg berries did not allay this gnawing, while they made his tongue and the roof of his mouth sore with their irritating bite.

He came upon a valley where rock ptarmigan

rose on whirring wings from the ledges and mus-
kegs. Ker — ker — ker was the cry they made.
He threw stones at them, but could not hit them.
He placed his pack on the ground and stalked them
as a cat stalks a sparrow. The sharp rocks cut
through his pant legs till his knees left a trail of
blood; but the hurt was lost in the hurt of his
hunger. He squirmed over the wet moss, saturating
his clothes and chilling his body; but he was not
aware of it, so great was his fever for food. And
always the ptarmigan rose, whirring, before him,
till their ker — ker — ker became a mock to him,
and he cursed them and cried aloud at them with
their own cry.

Once he crawled upon one that must have been
asleep. He did not see it till it shot up in his face
from its rocky nook. He made a clutch as startled
as was the rise of the ptarmigan, and there remained in his hand three tail-feathers. As he
watched its flight he hated it, as though it had
done him some terrible wrong. Then he returned
and shouldered his pack.

As the day wore along he came into valleys or
swales where game was more plentiful. A band
of caribou passed by, twenty-odd animals, tan-
talizingly within rifle range. He felt a wild desire
to run after them, a certitude that he could run
them down. A black fox came toward him, carrying

a ptarmigan in his mouth. The man shouted. It was a fearful cry, but the fox, leaping away in fright, did not drop the ptarmigan.

Late in the afternoon he followed a stream, milky with lime, which ran through sparse patches of rush grass. Grasping these rushes firmly near the root, he pulled up what resembled a young onion sprout no larger than a shingle nail. It was tender, and his teeth sank into it with a crunch that promised deliciously of food. But its fibers were tough. It was composed of stringy filaments saturated with water, like the berries, and devoid of nourishment. He threw off his pack and went into the rush grass on hands and knees, crunching and munching, like some bovine creature.

He was very weary and often wished to rest — to lie down and sleep; but he was continually driven on — not so much by his desire to gain the land of little sticks as by his hunger. He searched little ponds for frogs and dug up the earth with his nails for worms, though he knew in spite that neither frogs nor worms existed so far north.

He looked into every pool of water vainly until, as the long twilight came on, he discovered a solitary fish, the size of a minnow, in such a pool. He plunged his arm in up to the shoulder, but it eluded him. He reached for it with both hands and stirred up the milky mud at the bottom. In his excitement he fell in, wetting himself to the waist. Then the water was too muddy to admit of his seeing the fish, and he was compelled to wait until the sediment had settled.

The pursuit was renewed, till the water was again muddied. But he could not wait. He unstrapped the tin bucket and began to bale the pool. He baled wildly at first, splashing himself and flinging the water so short a distance that it ran back into the pool. He worked more carefully, striving to be cool, though his heart was pounding against his chest and his hands were trembling. At the end of half an hour the pool was nearly dry. Not a cupful of water remained. And there was no fish. He found a hidden crevice among the stones through which it had escaped to the adjoining and larger pool — a pool which he could not empty in a night and a day. Had he known of the crevice, he could have closed it with a rock at the beginning and the fish would have been his.

Thus he thought, and crumpled up and sank down upon the wet earth. At first he cried softly to himself, then he cried loudly to the pitiless desolation that ringed him around; and for a long time after he was shaken by great dry sobs.

He built a fire and warmed himself by drinking quarts of hot water, and made camp on a rocky ledge in the same fashion he had the night before.

The last thing he did was to see that his matches were dry and to wind his watch. The blankets were wet and clammy. His ankle pulsed with pain. But he knew only that he was hungry, and through his restless sleep he dreamed of feasts and banquets and of food served and spread in all imaginable ways.

He awoke chilled and sick. There was no sun. The gray of earth and sky had become deeper, more profound. A raw wind was blowing, and the first flurries of snow were whitening the hilltops. The air about him thickened and grew white while he made a fire and boiled more water. It was wet snow — half rain — and the flakes were large and soggy. At first they melted as soon as they came in contact with the earth, but ever more fell, covering the ground, putting out the fire, spoiling his supply of moss fuel.

This was a signal for him to strap on his pack and stumble onward, he knew not where. He was not concerned with the land of little sticks, nor with Bill and the cache under the upturned canoe by the river Dease. He was mastered by the verb "to eat." He was hunger-mad. He took no heed of the course he pursued, so long as that course led him through the swale bottoms. He felt his way through the wet snow to the watery muskeg berries, and went by feel as he pulled up the rush grass by the roots. But it was tasteless stuff and did not satisfy. He found a weed that tasted sour and he ate all he could find of it, which was not much, for it was a creeping growth, easily hidden under the several inches of snow.

He had no fire that night, nor hot water, and crawled under his blanket to sleep the broken hunger-sleep. The snow turned into a cold rain. He awakened many times to feel it falling on his upturned face. Day came — a gray day and no sun. It had ceased raining. The keenness of his hunger had departed. Sensibility, as far as concerned the yearning for food, had been exhausted. There was a dull, heavy ache in his stomach, but it did not bother him so much. He was more rational, and once more he was chiefly interested in the land of little sticks and the cache by the river Dease.

He ripped the remnant of one of his blankets into strips and bound his bleeding feet. Also, he recinched the injured ankle and prepared himself for a day of travel. When he came to his pack, he paused long over the squat moose-hide sack, but in the end it went with him.

The snow had melted under the rain, and only the hilltops showed white. The sun came out, and he succeeded in locating the points of the compass, though he knew now that he was lost. Perhaps, in his previous days' wanderings, he had edged away too far to the left. He now bore off to the right to counteract the possible deviation from his true course.

Though the hunger pangs were no longer so exquisite, he realized that he was weak. He was compelled to pause for frequent rests, when he attacked the muskeg berries and rush-grass patches. His tongue felt dry and large, as though covered with a fine hairy growth, and it tasted bitter in his mouth. His heart gave him a great deal of trouble. When he had traveled a few minutes it would begin a remorseless thump, thump, thump, and then leap up and away in a painful flutter of beats that choked him and made him go faint and dizzy.

In the middle of the day he found two minnows in a large pool. It was impossible to bale it, but he was calmer now and managed to catch them in his tin bucket. They were no longer than his little finger, but he was not particularly hungry. The dull ache in his stomach had been growing duller and fainter. It seemed almost that his stomach was dozing. He ate the fish raw, masticating with painstaking care, for the eating was an act of pure reason. While he had no desire to eat, he knew that he must eat to live.

In the evening he caught three more minnows, eating two and saving the third for breakfast. The sun had dried stray shreds of moss, and he was able to warm himself with hot water. He had not covered more than ten miles that day; and the next day, traveling whenever his heart permitted him, he covered no more than five miles. But his stomach did not give him the slightest uneasiness. It had gone to sleep. He was in a strange country, too, and the caribou were growing more plentiful, also the wolves. Often their yelps drifted across the desolation, and once he saw three of them slinking away before his path.

Another night; and in the morning, being more rational, he untied the leather string that fastened the squat moose-hide sack. From its open mouth poured a yellow stream of coarse gold dust and nuggets. He roughly divided the gold in halves, caching one half on a prominent ledge, wrapped in a piece of blanket, and returning the other half to the sack. He also began to use strips of the one remaining blanket for his feet. He still clung to his gun, for there were cartridges in that cache by the river Dease.

This was a day of fog, and this day hunger awoke in him again. He was very weak and was afflicted with a giddiness which at times blinded him. It was no uncommon thing now for him to stumble and fall; and stumbling once, he fell squarely into a ptarmigan nest. There were four newly hatched chicks, a day old — little specks of pulsating life no more than a mouthful — and he ate them ravenously, thrusting them alive into his mouth and crunching them like eggshells between his teeth. The mother ptarmigan beat about him with great outcry. He used his gun as a club with which to knock her over, but she dodged out of reach. He threw stones at her and with one chance shot broke a wing. Then she fluttered away, running, trailing the broken wing, with him in pursuit.

The little chicks had no more than whetted his appetite. He hopped and bobbed clumsily along on his injured ankle, throwing stones and screaming hoarsely at times; at other times hopping and bobbing silently along, picking himself up grimly and patiently when he fell, or rubbing his eyes with his hand when the giddiness threatened to overpower him.

The chase led him across swampy ground in the bottom of the valley, and he came upon footprints in the soggy moss. They were not his own — he could see that. They must be Bill's. But he could not stop, for the mother ptarmigan was running on. He would catch her first, then he would return and investigate.

He exhausted the mother ptarmigan; but he exhausted himself. She lay panting on her side. He lay panting on his side, a dozen feet away, unable to crawl to her. And as he recovered she recovered, fluttering out of reach as his hungry hand went out to her. The chase was resumed. Night settled down and she escaped. He stumbled from weakness and pitched head foremost on his face, cutting his cheek, his pack upon his back. He did not move for a long while; then he rolled over on his side, wound his watch, and lay there until morning.

Another day of fog. Half of his last blanket had gone into foot wrappings. He failed to pick up Bill's trail. It did not matter. His hunger was driving him too compellingly — only — only he wondered if Bill, too, were lost. By midday the irk of his pack became too oppressive. Again he divided the gold, this time merely spilling half of it on the ground. In the afternoon he threw the rest of it away, there remaining to him only the half-blanket, the tin bucket, and the rifle.

A hallucination began to trouble him. He felt confident that one cartridge remained to him. It was in the chamber of the rifle and he had overlooked it. On the other hand, he knew all the time that the chamber was empty. But the hallucination persisted. He fought it off for hours, then threw his rifle open and was confronted with emptiness. The disappointment was as bitter as though he had really expected to find the cartridge.

He plodded on for half an hour, when the hallucination arose again. Again he fought it, and still it persisted, till for very relief he opened his rifle to unconvince himself. At times his mind wandered farther afield, and he plodded on, a mere automaton, strange conceits and whimsicalities gnawing at his brain like worms. But these excursions out of the real were of brief duration, for ever the pangs of the hunger bite called him back. He was jerked back abruptly once from such an excursion by a sight that caused him nearly to faint. He reeled and swayed, doddering like a drunken man to keep from falling. Before him stood a horse. A horse! He could not believe his eyes. A thick mist was in them, intershot with sparkling points of light. He rubbed his eyes savagely to clear his vision, and beheld, not a horse, but a great brown bear. The animal was studying him with bellicose curiosity.

The man had brought his gun halfway to his shoulder before he realized. He lowered it and drew his hunting knife from its beaded sheath at his hip. Before him was meat and life. He ran his thumb along the edge of his knife. It was sharp. The point was sharp. He would fling himself upon the bear and kill it. But his heart began its warning thump, thump, thump. Then followed the wild upward leap and tattoo of flutters, the pressing as

233

of an iron band about his forehead, the creeping of the dizziness into his brain.

His desperate courage was evicted by a great surge of fear. In his weakness, what if the animal attacked him? He drew himself up to his most imposing stature, gripping the knife and staring hard at the bear. The bear advanced clumsily a couple of steps, reared up, and gave vent to a tentative growl. If the man ran, he would run after him; but the man did not run. He was animated now with the courage of fear. He too growled savagely, terribly, voicing the fear that is to life germane and that lies twisted about life's deepest roots.

The bear edged away to one side, growling menacingly, himself appalled by this mysterious creature that appeared upright and unafraid. But the man did not move. He stood like a statue till the danger was past, when he yielded to a fit of trembling and sank down into the wet moss.

He pulled himself together and went on, afraid now in a new way. It was not the fear that he should die passively from lack of food, but that he should be destroyed violently before starvation had exhausted the last particle of the endeavor in him that made toward surviving. There were the wolves. Back and forth across the desolation drifted their howls, weaving the very air into a fabric of menace that was so tangible that he found

himself, arms in the air, pressing it back from him
as if it might be the walls of a windblown tent.

Now and again the wolves, in packs of two and
three, crossed his path. But they sheered clear of
him. They were not in sufficient numbers, and
besides they were hunting the caribou, which did
not battle, while this strange creature that walked
erect might scratch and bite.

In the late afternoon he came upon scattered
bones where the wolves had made a kill. The
debris had been a caribou calf an hour before,
squawking and running and very much alive. He
contemplated the bones, clean-picked and polished,
pink with the cell-life in them which had not yet
died. Could it possibly be that he might be that ere
the day was done! Such was life, eh? A vain and
fleeting thing. It was only life that pained. There
was no hurt in death. To die was to sleep. It meant
cessation, rest. Then why was he not content to die?

But he did not moralize long. He was squatting
in the moss, a bone in his mouth, sucking at the
shreds of life that still dyed it faintly pink. The
sweet meaty taste, thin and elusive almost as a
memory, maddened him. He closed his jaws on
the bones and crunched. Sometimes it was the
bone that broke, sometimes his teeth. Then he
crushed the bones between rocks, pounded them
to a pulp, and swallowed them. He pounded his

fingers too in his haste, and yet found a moment in which to feel surprise at the fact that his fingers did not hurt much when caught under the descending rock.

Came frightful days of snow and rain. He did not know when he made camp, when he broke camp. He traveled in the night as much as in the day. He rested wherever he fell, crawled on whenever the dying life in him flickered up and burned less dimly. He, as a man, no longer strove. It was the life in him, unwilling to die, that drove him on. He did not suffer. His nerves had become blunted, numb, while his mind was filled with weird visions and delicious dreams.

But ever he sucked and chewed on the crushed bones of the caribou calf, the least remnants of which he had gathered up and carried with him. He crossed no more hills or divides, but automatically followed a large stream which flowed through a wide and shallow valley. He did not see this stream or this valley. He saw nothing save visions. Soul and body walked or crawled side by side, yet apart, so slender was the thread that bound them.

He awoke in his right mind, lying on his back on a rocky ledge. The sun was shining bright and warm. Afar off he heard the squawking of caribou calves. He was aware of vague memories of rain and wind and snow, but whether he had been beaten by the storm for two days or two weeks he did not know.

For some time he lay without movement, the genial sunshine pouring upon him and saturating his miserable body with its warmth. A fine day, he thought. Perhaps he could manage to locate himself. By a painful effort he rolled over on his side. Below him flowed a wide and sluggish river. Its unfamiliarity puzzled him. Slowly he followed it with his eyes, winding in wide sweeps among the bleak, bare hills, bleaker and barer and lower-lying than any hills he had yet encountered. Slowly, deliberately, without excitement or more than the most casual interest, he followed the course of the strange stream toward the skyline and saw it emptying into a bright and shining sea. He was still unexcited. Most unusual, he thought, a vision or a mirage — more likely a vision — a trick of his disordered mind. He was confirmed in this by sight of a ship lying at anchor in the midst of the shining sea. He closed his eyes for a while, then opened them. Strange how the vision persisted! Yet not strange. He knew there were no seas or ships in the heart of the barren lands, just as he had known there was no cartridge in the empty rifle.

He heard a snuffle behind him — a half-choking gasp or cough. Very slowly, because of his exceeding weakness and stiffness, he rolled over on his other side. He could see nothing near at hand, but he waited patiently. Again came the snuffle and cough, and outlined between two jagged rocks not a score of feet away he made out the gray head of a wolf. The sharp ears were not pricked so sharply as he had seen them on other wolves; the eyes were bleared and bloodshot, the head seemed to droop limply and forlornly. The animal blinked continually in the sunshine. It seemed sick. As he looked, it snuffled and coughed again.

This, at least, was real, he thought, and turned on the other side so that he might see the reality of the world which had been veiled from him before by the vision. But the sea still shone in the distance and the ship was plainly discernible. Was it reality, after all? He closed his eyes for a long while and thought, and then it came to him. He had been making north by east, away from the Dease Divide and into the Coppermine Valley. This wide and sluggish river was the Coppermine. That shining sea was the Arctic Ocean. That ship was a whaler, strayed east, far east, from the mouth of the Mackenzie, and it was lying at anchor in Coronation Gulf. He remembered the Hudson Bay Company chart he had seen long ago, and it was all clear and reasonable to him.

He sat up and turned his attention to immediate

affairs. He had worn through the blanket-wrappings, and his feet were shapeless lumps of raw meat. His last blanket was gone. Rifle and knife were both missing. He had lost his hat somewhere, with the bunch of matches in the band, but the matches against his chest were safe and dry inside the tobacco pouch and oil paper. He looked at his watch. It marked eleven o'clock and was still running. Evidently he had kept it wound.

He was calm and collected. Though extremely weak, he had no sensation of pain. He was not hungry. The thought of food was not even pleasant to him, and whatever he did was done by his reason alone. He ripped off his pant legs to the knees and bound them about his feet. Somehow he had succeeded in retaining the tin bucket. He would have some hot water before he began what he foresaw was to be a terrible journey to the ship.

His movements were slow. He shook as with palsy. When he started to collect dry moss, he found he could not rise to his feet. He tried again and again, then contented himself with crawling about on hands and knees. Once he crawled near the sick wolf. The animal dragged itself reluctantly out of his way, licking its chops with a tongue which seemed hardly to have the strength to curl. The man noticed that the tongue was not the customary healthy red. It was a yellowish brown and seemed coated with a rough and half-dry mucus.

After he had drunk a quart of hot water the man found he was able to stand, and even to walk as well as a dying man might be supposed to walk. Every minute or so he was compelled to rest. His steps were feeble and uncertain, just as the wolf's that trailed him were feeble and uncertain; and that night, when the shining sea was blotted out by blackness, he knew he was nearer to it by no more than four miles.

Throughout the night he heard the cough of the sick wolf, and now and then the squawking of the caribou calves. There was life all around him, but it was strong life, very much alive and well, and he knew the sick wolf clung to the sick man's trail in the hope that the man would die first. In the morning, on opening his eyes, he beheld it regarding him with a wistful and hungry stare. It stood crouched, tail between its legs, like a miserable and woebegone dog. It shivered in the chill morning wind, and grinned dispiritedly when the man spoke to it in a voice that achieved no more than a hoarse whisper.

The sun rose brightly, and all morning the man tottered and fell toward the ship on the shining sea. The weather was perfect. It was the brief Indian summer of the high latitudes. It might last a week. Tomorrow or next day it might be gone.

In the afternoon the man came upon a trail. It was of another man, who did not walk, but who dragged himself on all fours. The man thought it might be Bill, but he thought in a dull, uninterested way. He had no curiosity. In fact, sensation and emotion had left him. He was no longer susceptible to pain. Stomach and nerves had gone to sleep. Yet the life that was in him drove him on. He was very weary, but it refused to die. It was because it refused to die that he still ate muskeg berries and minnows, drank his hot water, and kept a wary eye on the sick wolf.

He followed the trail of the other man who dragged himself along, and soon came to the end of it — a few fresh-picked bones where the soggy moss was marked by the footpads of many wolves. He saw a squat moose-hide sack, mate to his own, which had been torn by sharp teeth. He picked it up, though its weight was almost too much for his feeble fingers. Bill had carried it to the last. Ha! ha! He would have the laugh on Bill. He could survive and carry it to the ship in the shining sea. His mirth was hoarse and ghastly, like a raven's croak, and the sick wolf joined him, howling lugubriously. The man ceased suddenly. How could he have the laugh on Bill if that were Bill; those bones, so pinky-white and clean, were Bill?

He turned away. Well, Bill had deserted him; but he would not take the gold, nor would he suck Bill's bones. Bill would have, though, had it been the other way around, he mused as he staggered on.

He came to a pool of water. Stooping over in quest of minnows, he jerked his head back as though he had been stung. He had caught sight of his reflected face. So horrible was it that sensibility awoke long enough to be shocked. There were three minnows in the pool, which was too large to drain; and after several ineffectual attempts to catch them in the tin bucket he forbore. He was afraid, because of his great weakness, that he might fall in and drown. It was for this reason that he did not trust himself to the river astride one of the many drift-logs which lined its sandpits.

That day he decreased the distance between him and the ship by three miles; the next day by two — for he was crawling now as Bill had crawled; and the end of the fifth day found the ship still seven miles away and him unable to make even a mile a day. Still the Indian summer held on, and he continued to crawl and faint, turn and turn about; and ever the sick wolf coughed and wheezed at his heels. His knees had become raw meat like his feet, and though he padded them with the shirt from his back it was a red track he left behind him on the moss and stones. Once, glancing back, he saw the wolf licking hungrily his bleeding trail, and he saw sharply what his own end might be — unless — unless he could get the wolf. Then began as grim a tragedy of existence as was ever played — a sick man that crawled, a sick wolf that limped, two creatures dragging their dying carcasses across the desolation and hunting each other's lives.

Had it been a well wolf, it would not have mattered so much to the man; but the thought of going to feed the maw of that loathsome and all-but-dead thing was repugnant to him. He was finicky. His mind had begun to wander again, and to be perplexed by hallucinations, while his lucid intervals grew rarer and shorter.

He was awakened once from a faint by a wheeze close in his ear. The wolf leaped lamely back, losing its footing and falling in its weakness. It was ludicrous, but he was not amused. Nor was he even afraid. He was too far gone for that. But his mind was for the moment clear, and he lay and considered. The ship was no more than four miles away. He could see it quite distinctly when he rubbed the mists out of his eyes, and he could see the white sail of a small boat cutting the water of the shining sea. But he could never crawl those four miles. He knew that, and was very calm in the knowledge. He knew that he could not crawl half a mile. And yet he wanted to live. It was unreasonable that he should die after all he had undergone. Fate asked too much of him. And, dying, he declined to die. It was stark madness, perhaps, but in the very grip of death he defied death and refused to die.

He closed his eyes and composed himself with infinite precaution. He steeled himself to keep above the suffocating languor that lapped like a rising tide through all the wells of his being. It was very like a sea, this deadly languor, that rose and rose and drowned his consciousness bit by bit. Sometimes he was all but submerged, swimming through oblivion with a faltering stroke; and again, by some strange alchemy of soul, he would find another shred of will and strike out more strongly.

Without movement he lay on his back, and he could hear, slowly drawing near and nearer, the wheezing intake and output of the sick wolf's breath. It drew closer, ever closer, through an infinity of time, and he did not move. It was at his ear. The harsh dry tongue grated like sandpaper against his cheek. His hands shot out — or at least he willed them to shoot out. The fingers were curved like talons, but they closed on empty air. Swiftness and certitude require strength, and the man had not this strength.

The patience of the wolf was terrible. The man's patience was no less terrible. For half a day he lay motionless, fighting off unconsciousness and waiting for the thing that was to feed upon him and upon which he wished to feed. Sometimes the languid sea rose over him and he dreamed long dreams; but ever through it all, waking and dreaming, he waited for the wheezing breath and the harsh caress of the tongue.

He did not hear the breath, and he slipped slowly from some dream to the feel of the tongue along his hand. He waited. The fangs pressed softly; the pressure increased; the wolf was exerting its last strength in an effort to sink teeth in the food for which it had waited so long. But the man had waited long, and the lacerated hand closed on the jaw. Slowly, while the wolf struggled feebly and the hand clutched feebly, the other hand crept across to a grip. Five minutes later the whole weight of the man's body was on top of the wolf. The hands had not sufficient strength to choke the wolf, but the face of the man was pressed close to the throat of the wolf and the mouth of the man was full of hair. At the end of half an hour the man was aware of a warm trickle in his throat. It was not pleasant. It was like molten lead being forced into his stomach, and it was

forced by his will alone. Later the man rolled over
on his back and slept.

There were some members of a scientific expedition on the whaling ship *Bedford*. From the deck
they remarked a strange object on the shore. It
was moving down the beach toward the water.
They were unable to classify it, and, being scientific
men, they climbed into the whaleboat alongside and
went ashore to see. And they saw something that
was alive but which could hardly be called a man.
It was blind, unconscious. It squirmed along the
ground like some monstrous worm. Most of its
efforts were ineffectual, but it was persistent, and it
writhed and twisted and went ahead perhaps a
score of feet an hour.

Three weeks afterward the man lay in a bunk
on the whaling ship *Bedford,* and with tears
streaming down his wasted cheeks told who he was
and what he had undergone. He also babbled inco-
herently of his mother, of sunny southern California, and a home among the orange groves and
flowers.

The days were not many after that when he sat
at table with the scientific men and ship's officers.
He gloated over the spectacle of so much food,
watching it anxiously as it went into the mouths of

others. With the disappearance of each mouthful an expression of deep regret came into his eyes. He was quite sane, yet he hated those men at mealtime. He was haunted by a fear that the food would not last. He inquired of the cook, the cabin boy, the captain, concerning the food stores. They reassured him countless times; but he could not believe them, and pried cunningly about the storeroom to see with his own eyes.

It was noticed that the man was getting fat. He grew stouter with each day. The scientific men shook their heads and theorized. They limited the man at his meals, but still his girth increased and he swelled prodigiously under his shirt.

The sailors grinned. They knew. And when the scientific men set a watch on the man, they knew too. They saw him slouch for'ard after breakfast, and, like a mendicant, with outstretched palm, accost a sailor. The sailor grinned and passed him a fragment of sea biscuit. He clutched it avariciously, looked at it as a miser looks at gold, and thrust it into his shirt bosom. Similar were the donations from other grinning sailors.

The scientific men were discreet. They let him alone. But they privily examined his bunk. It was lined with hardtack; the mattress was stuffed with hardtack; every nook and cranny was filled with hardtack. Yet he was sane. He was taking precautions against another possible famine — that was all. He would recover from it, the scientific men said; and he did, ere the *Bedford's* anchor rumbled down in San Francisco Bay.